DANDY DAY

Other books by Annie Wood

Just a Theory
Girl in the Whirl

Visit us online at
www.SpeakingVolumes.us

DANDY DAY

Annie Wood

SPEAKING VOLUMES, LLC
NAPLES, FLORIDA
2018

DANDY DAY

ISBN 978-1-62815-917-2

Dedicated to YOU.
All of you.
Thank you so much for your support
and encouragement.

Thank you for reminding me how much humans rock.

Acknowledgments

Be Bold and Mighty Forces Will Come to Your Aid.
—Goethe

It Takes Courage to Grow Up and Become Who You Really Are.
—E.E. Cummings

The Way to Happiness Sometimes Starts by Simply Waking the Hell Up.
—Annie Wood

Keep Creating.
Keep Positive.
Keep Showing Up.

Love and Peace
— Annie Wood

Chapter One

Dandy:

I'm in the middle of a field, with my arms out-stretched. It starts with Robert Downey Jr., then Johnny Depp, quickly followed by Colin Farrell, Bradley Cooper, and then Hugh Jackman. They all come raining down upon me from the sky, each one trapped inside their own personal raindrop. I feel like I can catch them all, *save* them all, and then, by doing so, save myself. I reach out my arms, preparing to gather the man-droplets, but something goes horribly wrong. They are much heavier than I expected, and it turns out the raindrops are made of glass. The weight of the droplets is just too much for me, so I drop them and then watch in horror as they loudly crash to the ground. Bradley, Hugh, Colin, all of them shatter into a million little pieces right before my very eyes. All because I wasn't able to hold on.

I think about crying, but instead...

I wake up.

My alarm clock is playing the same tune it always plays, *I Know Something About Love.* I'm a fan of irony. My recurring raining-men dream doesn't bother me so much anymore. I've grown accustomed to it. Although, there's always a moment, when I'm watching them slip through my fingers, where I'm deeply saddened. Saddened because I know it's inevitable.

The crash.

The shatter.

The end.

I grab my breakfast, which consists of one large chocolate Yoo-Hoo, and I put on my roller skates. I remind myself to try a strawberry Yoo-Hoo one day to shake things up a bit. It's another sunny day on the Venice boardwalk, and I'm ready to skate on over to my head-shrinking visit. Why am I getting my head shrunk? Because I live in Los Angeles. It's what we do here. Besides, my health insurance covers it, and I was curious as to what my subconscious is up to. Mostly about men. I love men. I think they love me, but, seemingly, just in small bursts, then, "POOF" the love is gone. I can't seem to make a relationship stick. I'm thirty-five years old. I'd really like one to stick.

Most of my life I've been floating about, having fun, exploring. I'm what they call a "free spirit." If I were speaking out loud now, I would have totally done the whole air quotes thing, except I'm glad that I didn't, because that's played-out. (Still, air quotes are *implied.)* Because the thing is, as much as I know that "free spirit" is not an insult, it usually comes off the heels of me doing something really stupid, like falling in-love with a guy because he has nicely sculpted eyebrows, or falling into an indoor swimming pool at a fancy-schmancy dinner party, or falling flat on my face while roller skating down the boardwalk. It would appear that I do an awful lot of falling. Anyway, I know what *they* mean by "free spirit." They mean: *wild, out of control, arrested development, woman-child, floozy.* And, maybe they're right. I like to make my own rules, which would explain why I don't have a real job. Okay, waitressing is a real job but not the way I do it. I wear roller skates all day, and the boss is a total groovy-hippie-type, so I am rarely held accountable for the orders I screw up and the dishes I break (both are plentiful). Roller skating around while balancing plates of grub isn't the easiest gig for the gravity-challenged, like myself, but it's certainly not the most challenging job either. Thirty-five years old.

I like to repeat the number in my head sometimes, *Thirty-five, thirty-five, thirty-five, thirty-five.* I repeat it to see if it will take shape in my mind and form into something concrete. What does this particular number mean? What did I imagine my life would be like at thirty-five? I'm not exactly mid-life unless I live to seventy; then, I am right smack in the middle. Maybe I am middle aged right now! Although my gramps is ninety-five, so if I make it that far, I'm still just a baby. My mom died when

I was eight, so that means she was only… thirty-five years old. Hang on a second… *I am currently the same age that my mom was when she died.* Whoa.

That's probably what subconsciously brought me to the therapist's office earlier this year. My "living in the moment" has brought me smack into this moment, which isn't horrible, but it's not much of anything, really. I work with my female bestie, Debbie, and I live next door to my male bestie, Simon. I work and hang out on the Venice boardwalk. I visit gramps once a week, but other than that, I'm kind of just… *being.* Either I'm super spiritual or super lazy. Doc Karen always asks me if I'm happy. I *think* I'm happy, but how can I tell?

I'm not *un*happy.

Is the absence of unhappiness, happiness?

I would enjoy a relationship, someone to share my life with.

But maybe I don't get to have that.

Doc Karen asks me how I feel about being thirty-five. I don't know what my age is supposed to mean, but I do know that it's important, because people are always talking about how old they are, how young they are, how much time they think they have left to do all of the things that they "should be doing by now." I find numbers to be exhausting. There's so much worry and fear behind them. Why don't we all just concentrate on living our lives, enjoying ourselves, maybe do some good things here and there and forget about the number that comes after our name? That oh-so important number is always taking center stage. Whenever I read a magazine article, the story always lists the names of people, followed immediately by their age. Blanche Smith, 47. Richard Donner, 23. Stella Burnside, 59. Why is that? Why don't they list useful information, Blanche Smith, hideous narcissist? Richard Donner, pathological liar. Stella Burnside, greedy gold-digger. Those paint a much more interesting picture than a couple of silly numbers.

"Hey Dandy! Late again?" Simon yells from his window.

"I'm nothing if not consistent!" I yell back at him.

We often yell back at forth like this, Simon and I. He's been my boy bestie since we were eleven years old, growing up in the San Fernando Valley. His is the shoulder I cried on when gramps picked me up from school that day. Gramps was crying hard as he tried to tell me about the accident. I had never seen a grown-up cry before. It was horrible. As he told me about my mother, his daughter's, death, I remember my little arms wrapping around my big, survivor grandpa's shoulders and telling him that it will be okay. My dad ran away from home when I was a baby, now my mom was gone, and my grandmother died before I was born. It was just me and gramps now. I didn't cry until Simon came over that day to play. Simon didn't know what to do, but he let me hug him while I cried, and I remember him patting my head a few times. I felt so close to Simon in that moment; even though we were only kids, I thought to myself, "please don't ever go away." And as luck would have it, Simon is the only man, other than gramps, that hasn't gone away.

Simon's also thirty-five, but he doesn't seem too concerned about it. He's never been married and has absolutely nothing figured out about his life either. He's a bartender at a cool, historic bar in Venice called *Zane's*. It used to be a speakeasy in the twenties. Ah, the twenties. I've always had the sneaking suspicion that I was a flapper in a past life. It must have been a great time with all of that dancing, champagne drinking and fun! Except for the market crashing, the poverty, and prohibition. Well, good with the bad, right?

Anyhow, Simon is a great barkeep. He's a master mixologist. He's also a really good writer, but he spends more time mixing than writing.

"Wanna grab a pizza later?" He asks me, knowing full well the answer.

"Duh." I wave up at him and then skate off for my head-shrinking.

On the way, The Ride-By Psychic passes me on his beat-up ten speed. He has an old fashioned, pink bell on the handlebars. The kind little girls have on their first bicycles. He rings it and startles me. "A tall man will give you a gift!" He yells at me as he zooms by, ringing his bell two more times. Ride-By Psychic's predictions are usually freakishly spot on.

I wave hello to Stilts-Guy who leans down and gives me a sunflower. Ride-By Psychic was right again! Stilts-Guy walks all around the boardwalk in mime face and on six foot stilts, but this is the first time he's giving me a gift. Maybe it's a positive sign of things to come. I smile and thank him and then turn to give a salute to Robot-Man. Robot-Man paints himself silver and stands in a tableau at various parts of the boardwalk. All of these guys are part of the local flavor in Venice and I love them. But not enough to learn their actual names.

I arrive at the office all sticky and sweaty from the skate over. I must remember to pack deodorant in my backpack.

"Hit snooze one too many times, did we?" Shelly snarks. Shelly is my shrink's secretary, and everything she says sounds snarky. Actually, too bad her last name isn't Snark. Shelly Snark has a ring to it. But it would get old fast. I know a little something about that.

"Dandy Day you should really discuss your compulsive lateness with the doctor," Shelly snarks some more.

"Will do," I lie.

"Wait!" she calls after me, "You should know that…"

I ignore Shelly and barge into the doc's office. It turns out that my Doctor is, in fact, *not* in. In her place is… some guy.

"Good morning, Dandy, I'm Dr. Bill Greenberg, but most of my patients call me Dr. Bill." He smiles at me with a smile that I know is supposed to calm me but actually creeps me out. Then he simultaneously waves and winks at me, super slowly.

"Where's Karen?"

"Well, Dr. Hurdling had a family emergency. I'm filling in for her until she returns. Is that okay?"

"She left? Just like that. I mean, she can do that?"

Dr. Bill points to a chair as if he was doing Tai Chi. Jeez, everything is slow and deliberate with this guy. Hurry it up, weirdo.

"Please, have a seat, Miss Day."

I sit down. I think I'm in shock. "Where did she go?"

"Family emergency. That's all I know."

I know that when I hear that someone has a family emergency that I'm supposed to inquire about them. I'm supposed to hope that everything is okay and wish her well and maybe even send her a card and flowers or something. But I rant instead.

"I can't believe she would do this to me. She knows I have abandonment issues and she just dumps me, with no text, no email, no notice whatsoever or reason, she leaves me with a... *man.*"

Dr. Bill smiles. "I'm flattered that you noticed."

"Yeah, well... it's just..."

"You feel that most of your problems *stem* from men so it would be awkward to try and explain this *to* a man?"

"Yeah, something like that."

"After all," he continues, "I am not so terrible to look at, and you most likely feel that there would be an underlying sexual tension that would hinder your level of comfort and could possibly get in the way of my honest analysis."

"Say what now?" Apparently my articulation was not enough to stop him.

He continues, "No need to dwell on these facts, Ms. Day. I assure you that my professionalism will remain intact."

"I don't feel any sexual tension."

"You don't need to feel ashamed."

"I'm not ashamed."

Dr. Bill takes out a note pad and begins writing furiously. "I think I can help you with your denial."

"I'm not in denial!"

"You are in denial about being in denial. Very common."

"Is this a joke? Are you nuts?"

"Placing blame. Name calling. Inability to take things seriously... I think we're on to something." He continues scribbling in his note pad.

"What are you doing? Is this going down on my permanent record? Stop taking notes!"

"Controlling, demanding..."

"Who set you up to this?" I demand to know.

"Paranoid," he says as he jots down more notes in his stupid notebook.

I'm a grown-up, and I don't have to listen to this guy's crap. He's not even my real head shrinker! I stand up and calmly say, "Under the circumstances, I feel that I should come back when my regular doctor returns."

"What circumstances?"

"I don't like you."

"I see." He looks down at his notebook, hurt.

I hate it when I'm responsible for someone being hurt. Crap.

"It's just that, Doc Karen and I were on the brink of figuring things out, and I just think..."

"What kind of things?" He really wants to know.

"Well, we were just about to tackle my little fear of intimacy thingie, but I felt that we were seeing too much of each other, so I stopped coming for awhile."

"Right."

"Then, I came back, and we were going to tackle my running away problem and my fear of abandonment. You know, before, she… abandoned me."

I start for the door again. He stops me with a crying plea, "Please, don't go!"

"Are you sure you're a doctor?"

"Why don't you just give it a try?" He points to the chair again.

I sit. I don't know what snaps in me that makes me decide to share anything with this bozo. Maybe the fact that "Dr. Bill" sounds a lot like "Dr. Phil," and I'm a devoted fan of the latter. I especially love all of Dr. Phil's catch phrases. *This ain't my first rodeo! That dog won't hunt!* And of course, everyone's favorite, *how's that working for you?* I sort of have a thing for Dr. Phil. Did you know that bald guys have more testosterone than guys with a full head of hair? That means baldies are more virile, hormonally speaking. That could make them more passionate. I'd take virility & passion over wavy locks any day.

"Whenever you're ready," Dr. Bill says, clearing his throat.

"Well, for starters, all of my relationships seem to have a whopping three month life span."

"And?"

"And, that's not very long."

"You want longer relationships?"

"No, I don't want longer relationships. I want *one long relationship.* That works."

Dr. Bill studies me. He begins to squint his eyes, and I begin to mirror him. Now he appears blurry, and I feel like I'm tripping on mushrooms. I tried that once a few years ago with Simon." I remember Simon's hair started to drip to the ground like melted wax, and I was upset, because I thought that if anyone stepped in it that they would drown in his wax puddle of melted hair, and then the surviving members of their family would sue Simon for damages. Then, maybe Simon would have to go to jail, because he couldn't afford to pay the fine, and then I'd have to dress conservatively, like in turtle necks and prairie skirts when I would go to visit him, so the other prisoners wouldn't cat-call me when I walked down the aisle, and *turtle necks suffocate me!*

Yeah, I never took mushrooms again.

Dr. Bill interrupts my flashback. "Maybe you just haven't met the right fella."

I grimace while Dr. Bill, sensing that he's losing me, flips through my file, desperately searching for something. He's squirming now.

He finds something. "Ah ha! It says here that you have a problem with your name."

"Oh, right. I'm totally over that."

"Are you?" He leans in, the way he must have seen shrinks do on TV.

"I used to think that it was too much pressure being named *Dandy*. With my last name being *Day*. Like, I'm expected to always *have* a dandy day because I *am* Dandy Day. And then there's the annoying question of "how are you?" I can't say "fine," like everyone else gets to, no, no, I have to be careful that I am not 'fine *and* dandy.'

What the hell kind of name is Dandy anyway?"

Interesting. I could have sworn I had that button removed.

"Why don't you just change your name?" He asks.

"Then *they* win."

I think I'm confusing the poor guy. He keeps looking at me with that puzzled look on his face. "How often do you come in?" He asks me.

"Once a week."

"I think we should up it to three."

This time, I get up, and I mean it. I walk towards the exit.

"I think I'll just work on myself," I tell him.

"Oh, you can't do that," he says meaningfully.

"I can't?"

"No, you should leave it to the professionals."

"I can totally heal myself. People do it all the time! It's all the rage these days.

I can follow Chopra on twitter, watch the O network, do yoga and avoid gluten. I should be as right as rain in no time."

"It won't work!" He barks.

"Is this reverse psychology?" I say, with my hand on the doorknob.

Doc smiles and whispers, "Why don't we discuss this over a drink tonight?"

"Are you asking me out?"

"That's not okay, is it?"

Doc looks down, embarrassed.

It would appear that this is one shrink that desperately needs to be shrunk.

Chapter Two

Dandy:

Simon offers to kick the good doctor's ass. We are eating pizza on his sofa watching TV Land. This is what we do, Simon and I. In fact, it's what we've been doing for more than two decades now. We bonded big time in the fifth grade, when neither one of us were invited to Jamie Swanson's birthday party extravaganza. I say "extravaganza," because it was a little girl suburbia fantasy with pony rides and snow cone machines, the whole bit. Why weren't we invited? It turns out Jamie's mom had the hots for Simon's dad, but Simon's dad gave her the cold shoulder in favor of Carla Wrightwood's hotsty-totsy step-mom with the new boobs. But, as far as Jamie Swanson's duck lipped mamma was concerned, she was forever scorned. And you know what they say about hell, fury, and a woman scorned and all that. So, there we were, the only two kids in Mrs. Wright's fifth grade class *not* invited to the party of the century. Simon came over to my house, where we ate pizza and watched TV. I don't eat the crust. He loves the crust. So there it was. And there it remains.

We watched *Quantum Leap* every week together. We thought Sam, played by Scott Bakula, was a true hero, popping into people's lives and helping fix whatever was broken. We both agreed that Al, the hologram, played by Dean Stockwell was too gruff, and that Sam should fly solo. When they cancelled that show, we became obsessed with *Friends*. We totally identified with that show. Until they all started hooking up. We thought they should change the title to *Friends Who Now Hook Up, Fall in-Love and Make Babies.* But the acronym for that is too long. FWNHUFILMB. See?

So, here we are.

Still watching our shows.

Still eating a lot of pizza.

Still the best of friends.

"I'm serious. That is completely uncool for him to hit on you. Hasn't he heard of the whole #metoo movement? He's totally not paying attention. I wouldn't mind giving that loser a good talking to," Simon says between bites.

"A good talking to?" I laugh. "Yeah, you sound like a real tough guy. You're such a nerd."

"Nerd or not. The guy's a putz."

"Anyhow," I continue, "I'm sure he meant well. Poor guy, probably gets a lot of rejection."

"Poor guy? He's a doctor, he makes like, what, a gazillion bucks an hour?"

"Yeah, but he's a nutcase."

"He's a *rich* nut case. Maybe I should be a shrink. Tending bar is the same thing," Simon says as he starts on my discarded crusts.

I get up to grab a Yoo-Hoo. "I don't see why you're always so concerned with money."

"Oh? You don't?" Simon laughs. "Well, you'd be the first of your kind who doesn't."

Simon thinks women don't like him because he's "only a bartender." But I think he's looking in all the wrong places. Like, *a bar.* Not just any bar but the *only* bar he ever goes to, which happens to be the one he works at.

"Those girls you date are all screw-ups, if you ask me."

"I didn't."

"Those girls you date, they are not worthy of a guy like you."

"That's touching, but it's bullshit."

"It's not bullshit."

"It's touching bullshit."

"It's true. They don't appreciate a guy with character."

"Yeah, I always hear girls at the bar going on and on about how they want to go home with a guy with a lot of... *character.*"

"That's not the best place to meet someone of quality."

"This, coming from a relationship retard."

"Whoa! We don't use that word anymore!"

"You're right. I felt guilty as soon as I said it. A relationship... moron?"

"Better,' I say. "Well, Doc Karen was helping me with my moronic ways before she dumped me." I take a swig of my Yoo-Hoo like I'm Annie freakin Oakley and it's some, hard, tasty rye. I think about burping, but I've never been able to burp on cue.

"What was Doc Karen going to do that was so special?" Simon asks.

"She was going to help me examine my past relationships, so I would take notice of my patterns and learn how to not repeat them."

Simon leans back on the sofa and puts his feet up on my legs. "Sounds time consuming to me."

"I guess mental health is supposed to be time consuming."

I think long and hard about my past patterns while I watch Simon finish off the last of my pizza crusts.

Chapter Three

Dandy:

If I were born to like women in that way I would like my friend, Debbie, in that way. But, since I'm not, I can just intellectually and objectively say, by panning my proverbial camera back and observing her, that Debbie is the fantasy of many. She's the perfect combo of cute/sexy/crazy that makes for a lot of fun. She's my slightly sluttier, more cynical mirror. I didn't know Deb in the fifth grade, like I did Simon, but, if I had, I'm certain that *she* would have been invited to Jamie Swanson's epic party. Heck, she probably would have planned the damn thing and charge admission.

"I don't see what you need a psychologist for, anyway. Your mind is just fine as it is," Deb tells me on our way to work.

We often roller skate to work together, down the Venice boardwalk, usually trying to stay a good distance ahead of the local roller skating famous Krishna, Harry Perry. He plays his guitar while singing *Krishna*, (which is catchy but repetitive) and usually you can't get away from him unless you hand him a buck. But a buck a day adds up, so, we just try to skate faster.

"Because it's good to have someone to vent to," I explain.

"Just vent to me," she offers.

"Yeah, I tried that. You told me that when I'm feeling stressed, I should just picture everyone around me naked."

I don't have the heart to tell her, but I saw that *Brady Bunch* repeat too. The one where Mr. Brady tells Peter that if he gets nervous when he's giving a speech on stage that he should just picture the audience in their underwear. Or maybe it was Mrs. Brady who told Cindy. Or Alice. Or Tiger told Miss Kitty. I can't remember. But someone in that Brady household thought it up. It was a popular concept dating back to at least the 1970s, and it doesn't work.

"Have you tried it?" Deb asks me.

"No. It's stupid."

To our surprise, Harry Perry manages to catch up to us, and he's on our heels singing *Krishna* and playing his guitar.

"Hey Harry," we both mumble. He smiles. He's always smiling, so really he just *keeps* smiling.

The Ride-By Psychic rings his little bell and yells to me without slowing down, "You're going to live until age eighty-nine!"

"Ah Ha! So I am *not* middle aged!" I yell back at him, but he doesn't look back or respond. It's a very one-way relationship I have with The Ride-By Psychic.

Debbie continues, "You're too closed off. You have to try new things. No wonder your shrink dumped you." She pushes me, good naturedly, but since, as I previously mentioned, I'm an easy faller, like a rom com female protagonist trope, but I can't help myself, I fall straight into Harry, who falls back onto the ground with me on top of him. Amazingly, he doesn't miss a beat and never stops playing the guitar and singing, *Krishna, Krishna, Krishna...*

"Oh my God, I'm sorry!" Debbie gasps, as she comes to our rescue.

"It's okay, it's okay. I'm fine. Sorry, Harry." Both Debbie and I reach inside our purses and pull out a few dollar bills to hand to Harry. He takes them and skates off, singing all the while... *Haree Haree... Harree...*

Chapter Four

Simon:

That doctor of Dandy's wasn't helping her one bit. Not one bit. All she did was listen to her, which I've been doing, *for free*, for most of our lives. Sure, she gave her advice, which she never took, and told her things like, "I think we are making great progress," which was all a bunch of bull. What Dandy needs is simple. She needs to grow up, ask more of herself and let others in. Well not just anyone, just someone she trusts. I'm not saying that I want her to be different... it's just that... it wouldn't be all-together a terrible thing if she *behaved* a little differently. Not much differently... just... maybe she could slow down a bit and not overthink everything. Maybe she could see how good she's got it, you know? Of course, I'm probably "projecting" right now. Isn't that what they call it? I'm saying that *she* should be different in the exact ways that I think *I* should be different? I don't know, I've never been to therapy.

My mind trails off like this, thinking about Dandy, but I need to focus, since it's another

busy happy hour at the bar. Two sexy blondes are staring at me as I flip a few bottles. I juggle and show off just like Tom Cruise in *Cocktail*. The ladies eat this stuff up. I'm not an all-together terrible juggler.

"I love it when you do that, Simon," coos the tall blonde.

"Yeah, do it again," echoes the short blonde.

"I aim to please," I gloat, as I juggle the bottles higher in the air.

"I bet you never drop them," short blonde adds.

"No way, he's a pro," confirms tall blonde.

"Do you have a girlfriend?" They ask at the same time. I kid you not, *at the same time.*

"Uh, no... I'm sort of "in-between" girlfriends right now," I stammer, still juggling.

The tall blonde leans in closer and whispers, "how would you like to be "in-between" us?"

Crash!
Shatter!
There goes my perfect record.

The blondes crack up. Well, that's good. Chicks love funny guys, right?

"So, I get off at midnight," I offer.

"Yeah, well, we don't," the short one quips. And I thought she was the nice one.

They laugh and mock their way to the exit but first they throw down a twenty.

"Keep the change!" They shout back.

I bend down to clean up my massive mess. I know, I know, I'm a sucker for one pretty face, never mind two of them. I wouldn't mind it so much if the pretty faces came with a heart every once in awhile. Each time I swallow my pride, because I'm a hopeless romantic. Sometimes I think I should treat life like an ongoing *X-Files* episode. *Trust no one.* Actually, maybe I do treat life like an ongoing *X-Files* episode. I just chose the other tag line - *The Truth is Out There*.

My truth.

Out there.

Somewhere.

So, I keep looking.

I clean up the glass and then make myself an Old-Fashioned. I notice Dandy talking to the blondes. She's smiling. She's animated. Oh, this can't be good. I inconspicuously get myself closer, so I can listen in on their conversation.

"You guys are going to be late for the ball!" Dandy says to the blondes.

"Excuse me?" The tall one says.

Dandy continues, "You should be there to make sure Cinderella doesn't nab the prince."

The short blonde is confused. "There's a prince in town?"

The tall one nudges her. "No, stupid. She's screwing with us." They stare at Dandy. The tall one adds, "We don't like to be screwed with."

"Oh, sorry. Never mind. I thought you two knew," Dandy says mater-of-factly as she walks away from them and towards me. The blondes follow her.

"Knew what?" The tall one asks in her most faux nonchalant tone.

Dandy bellies up to the bar and smiles at me, the blondes at her heels. I make Dandy one of our drink specials, *Strawberry Fields*. Strawberry infused Pisco Torentel, cardamom, rose, citrus, sparkling wine. We do good work here. Dandy points to the bouncer and speaks secretively to the blondes. "Do you see that guy over there?"

"Yeah? So?" Says the tall one.

"Go over to him and say that you are 'ready to go to the ball.' It's the password for an exclusive invitation to Jay-Z's VIP private party."

"Really?" I can't tell if the tall one is in or if she's out.

"And that's where the prince will be?" The short one adds.

The tall one smacks the short one again. "There's no ball. They don't even have those anymore."

25

"Suit yourself," Dandy says. "But, that's where the prince and a bunch of other *rich,* available guys will be."

The short one drags the tall one over to the bouncer, giggling. Looks like the tall one is in after all. They whisper the password to the massive bouncer. He looks up and smiles at Dandy, then proceeds to escort the two blondes out the exit, kicking them to the curb.

Dandy sips her Strawberry Fields. "I told you not to talk to girls."

"Thanks, Dandy, but that wasn't necessary."

"Maybe not. But it sure was fun."

"Damn, this is goooooood." She says, enjoying her drink.

She's smiling ear to ear. A naughty without entirely losing the nice smile.

It's my favorite smile.

"Oh! I've got news!" She exclaims.

"Okay, shoot."

"I'm going to heal myself, and I have a plan!"

I settle in and take a sip of my Old Fashioned.

"So, who do you think might have some insight as to why I suck at relationships?"

"The Dalai Lama?"

"No! The people I've had relationships with. And also maybe the Dalai Lama, but I don't have his number."

"But you don't even keep in touch with your exes."

"No, but I'm sure I can find them. And then I'll ask them some pointed questions. I figure that if each of them has a *partial* idea as to why it didn't work out with them, then I could gather all of the pieces of information and put the puzzle together! And Presto! The big picture!" She concludes.

"Great. I'm happy for you." I tell her, as I polish off my Old Fashioned and make a slurpy sound with my straw. I continue to make this slurpy sound in lieu of saying anything more to her. I don't think this plan is so great. I mean, what if sparks reunite with one of them, and she ends up going backwards in her life, stuck with the wrong guy again? On the other hand, I don't want to be critical when she looks so proud of herself.

"It's just... have you considered that these were just not the right guys for you, and that is that?"

"That is that?" Dandy thinks for a second. "Nope. Can't be that simple." She whips out her iPhone and records into her recording app. "First subject to take part in *the project,* A one... Brent Walters of Santa Monica, California, age 33. Relationship was hot and heavy, very sexy, break-up due to... an argument of some kind? Maybe. I don't know. I forget exactly." Then she takes out a little notebook from her purse that already has a list of names.

She points to it. "I already have a list, see?"

"Yes, I see that."

Into her app, "I will contact Brent in 0 100 hours."

She doesn't even know what 0 100 hours is.

Okay, neither do I.

Chapter Five

Debbie:

Yes, I'm Dandy's bestie, and I have something to say about that. The role of "The Best Friend" is always played by a B or C lister. It's the not-as-cute-as-or-smart-as-the-star-but-still-sexy-funny-in-a quirky-way role. The second banana. Well, that ain't the case here. And I used the word ain't ironically. I know it's not a proper word. But *this* best friend is no second banana. I don't mean that in a bitchy, competitive way, I just mean that I am way too cute to be a sidekick.

I shared a joint with Dandy and Simon six years ago at a Bob Marley festival. I can't remember who originated the joint, but I do remember that the three of us were flying high and confessed that we never smoked pot before. How weird is that? All three of us, total pot virgins at a *Bob Marley festival?* We decide right then and there that it's kismet that we should all be friends. I got Dandy this job at the café, and she's managed to keep it, even though she's broken more dishes than she serves. I don't hang out with them as much as they hang out with one another. I mean, they have such a close friendship, it's difficult to penetrate it. I often feel like the third wheel when we are all together, so I pretty much just keep my friendship with Dandy in the confines of our job. Me and Simon have a great "Hey, what's up?" type of friendship. It doesn't go much deeper than that, and we like it that way.

Unlike many female friendships, I don't feel competitive with Dandy. I mean, we're different people, we want different things, and we have totally different taste in men, so that keeps things simple. Dandy likes to analyze everything, and I seldom analyze anything.

Dandy tells me all about her new "heal thyself" plan while we skate around work, setting up for the lunch crowd. I try to reason with her.

"I just don't get why you think they'll want to talk to you. It's not like they're your friends."

I've been non-stop dating since I was twelve years old, so this is a subject I am fluent in. The *only* subject I am fluent in. I explain to her that men, as a rule, are suspect of women with an agenda.

"What if I pay them fifty bucks?" Dandy asks.

"That should do it for the actor, but I'm not sure about the others."

I then explain to her how men like to know what they will *get* from what they *give*. And they are usually big fans of rules. Like in sports, war and sex.

"Deb, I need answers, so I have to ask questions."

I'm about to tell her that there's no shortage of shrinks in L.A., so she could easily find another, but customers are now coming in, so it's time to be all perky, bright eyed and bushy tailed. I skate over to the old-timer who was just seated at my table. I swing by and grab a coffee carafe first.

"Hey toots, how'd ya know?" Old timer smiles, as I pour him a cup of Joe.

"I'm good like that," I tell him.

CRASH! Dandy dropped something. Again.

"Dandy? You okay?" I yell from across the patio.

She can't seem to find the words. Instead she puts one hand in front of her mouth, and then, with the other, she points to table fourteen. I recognize him immediately. It's *Brent*. One of the exes on Dandy's list. Well, I guess this plan of hers has been set into motion by the powers that be. I motion to her to go over there. She looks like she might faint.

On second thought, this project of hers could be a lot of fun.

Chapter Six

Dandy:

Okay, I can do this. He's just a guy. A guy I used to bump uglies with, but still, just a guy. A guy who is seated at my section with a girl. His girl? Well, it's not his sister, I remember his sister, and that's not her. So, it could be his wife or girlfriend or maybe a first date. She has red hair. I guess that's sexy. Do guys like that? I don't know. I'm rambling inside my head, and if I don't stop, I'm afraid my head will burst all together, and that would cause a scene. And probably be painful. And messy. Okay, snap out of it, Dandy! Let's do this.

"OUCH!" I ram into a chair on my way over. Brent looks up and notices me for the first time.

"Dandy? Is that you?" He looks at me with shock and maybe a hint of embarrassment for me.

I fake a calm, cool, collected response. "Brent? Oh, hey, wow, long time no see."

"Are you okay?" Asks the red head.

"Yes, thank you. Fine… and dandy. Ha!" I think I'm playing it cool, but I don't play that very well.

"I can't believe you still work here. That's like a record for you, isn't it?" Brent jokes.

"Oh… right… exactly… totally." I stammer. "I actually really like it here. It's close to home, and the hours are great. I have tons of free time to do what I want."

"Which is?"

"Oh, to… you know... hang out." Yes, that is the best I could come up with.

"Still as ambitious as ever," Brent laughs and winks at Red. She smiles.

"Ambition is overrated!" I snap. "I'd rather be happy," I add feeling proud of my quick thinking.

"Can't you be both?" Asks Red.

"I don't know yet." I put out my hand towards Red. "I'm Dandy."

Red shakes my hand. "Roxanne."

And, shocking even myself, I begin to sing! *"Rooooxanne, you don't have to put on your red dress tonight…"*

Red forces a tiny grin in my direction. A pity grin.

Then there's that horrible, dreadful moment. That moment of silence.

"So..."

"So, how about some menus?" Asks Brent.

"Right. I'm on it!" I say, as I quickly skate away finding Debbie in the kitchen.

"Can you believe it?" I stage whisper intensely.

"I guess your project is meant to be. You should ask him your questions."

"Now?" I ask.

Debbie thrusts menus in my hands. "There's no time like the present."

I roll back to table fourteen, hand them their menus and proceed to stare at Brent. Waiting.

Brent looks up from the menus. "I'm not sure... we might need a few minutes..."

"Why did we break up?" I blurt.

"Excuse me?" Brent says, while Red looks at me with her disgruntled eyes stabbing me right through to my guts.

"It's just..." I continue, improvising... "I'm kind of doing this project, a self-discovery sort of thing, a why-don't-my-relationships-last-kind-of-thing, and I thought that you might have some insight on the subject, since we were going really hot and heavy for a while, and then..."

"I'll have a Greek salad." Red says. If words could kill, she would have killed me dead with *I'll have a Greek Salad.*

I apologize to Red. "I'm sorry, I know this is weird. I'm not still into him or anything. Oh God, no! You can have him!"

"Thanks," Brent says.

"I'll have a Pinot Grigio," Red says.

But I'm on a roll, and when I'm on a roll, I find it difficult to stop rolling. "I mean, I can't remember whose fault the break-up was or why it happened at all. It *couldn't* have been the sex; if I remember correctly, the sex was sensational."

"Make that a vodka tonic," Red says. "Hold the tonic." She's got a point. I'm overstaying my welcome in cray-cray town even for myself.

Brent finally speaks, "It was mutual. The break up."

Red addresses Brent now. "Honey, you don't have to play along with this... *waitress*."

Ouch. She called me a *waitress*. How dare she! She knows my name! True, I am calling her by the color of her hair, and I know her name as well. Still, "Red" is just a nickname, and I'm only calling her that in my head. She called me a "waitress" *out loud*.

I have a seat at their table. Maybe if I'm eye level, Red won't find me as overbearing. She continues to glare at me, while I concentrate on Brent. "We had a fight. I remember a fight."

Brent nods his head, remembering. "It was over laundry."

"I can't believe this." Red is getting all worked up. She crosses her arms in front of her chest and leans back in her chair, now glaring at us both.

"That's it!" I touch Brent's arm. "You're right! I remember now. The socks, something with the socks!"

Red gets up. "I'm out of here." I scoot my chair a bit to let her pass and wait for Brent to say something to her. But he doesn't seem to notice. Wow, what a putz. Red should totally leave his ass. But, I'm on a mission, so, I continue, "You didn't like the way I folded your socks!"

Brent is getting caught up in the memory now. "My mom rolled them. I prefer them rolled."

"That's right! I forgot, you're a mamma's boy."

"You see? It's cracks like that…" Brent snaps.

"You're a grown man, why should your girlfriend have to do things exactly the way your mother did?"

"It's just a preference! What's so wrong with having a preference? Why does everything have to be done your way!"

I'm standing now. "Maybe you should just roll your own God damn socks!"

Brent stands. "Maybe you're right!"

We are standing there, face to face now, super pissed-off and loud and fuming. We lock eyes in a stare-down that feels like it can never end. Now I remember everything about our story. I'm done here, and I lean one last time deeper into his eyes to spite him, his socks and his mother. He matches my stare, and before I know it, our mouths lock onto each other in a passionate kiss.

We hear a smattering of applause from my customers who are probably just happy that we are using our mouths for something other than yelling.

After a shocked moment I speak. "This didn't really help me."

"Okay. Also… you were controlling, unpredictable and..."

"Not enough like your mother?"

"Not enough like my mother."

I smile. He smiles.

After a moment, he looks around the table. "Hey, where did Roxanne go?"

Chapter Seven

Simon:

Dandy's half of the pizza has jalapeños on it. She loves her jalapeños. She pops them like my mom pops Xanax. I wonder if there's a connection between people who have a high tolerance for spicy foods with how much spice they prefer in their life. Dandy seems to attract fire, and she also seems to thrive in it. I prefer calm. I always have. When I was a kid, I used to tell my imaginary friends to use their inside voice. I don't like a lot of noise. Yet, Dandy is my best pal, and I seem to tolerate her just fine. Maybe I'm just used to her.

She crosses Brent off her list and smiles at me. "Moving on." She reaches for her iPhone and hits record. "Case study number two, Kevin Myers of West Hollywood, California, age 31, break-up due to…" she looks at me for help.

"Isn't he the one who just packed up and left?" I offer.

"No fight?" She asks.

"I think he left a note. Thank You."

"You're welcome."

"No, not you. That's what the *note* said. The note said, *Thank you.*"

"Oh, yeah," I remember. "It was weird."

Dandy reaches for another slice. "I asked for extra jal-apeños. There's never enough jalapeños."

The pizza is literally covered with the spicy, green pepper. Maybe she has no taste buds left. The many years of jalapeño-popping has burned them off.

"Wanna come with?" She asks me.

"No."

"Why?" She never just let's something lie.

"I have a date," I tell her. The truth is, I'm not really looking forward to it because I find dating to be stressful. Too much having to jump through hoops and pretending to be interested in things I'm not interested in, so I can appear... interested. Still, it's something to do. I have to keep busy. I have the feeling that I must do things or else my life will slip entirely away from me.

I often feel restless, as if there's something that I'm supposed to be doing, but I've forgotten what it is. Maybe it's - get a career and have a family.

So, I suppose I will start with - leave the house and date a girl.

"Another bar fly?"

"No," I say a bit defensively. "I met her at *Whole Foods*. I helped her decide which almond milk would go best with her organic corn puffs. "

"The vanilla."

"Definitely."

Dandy drops the pizza on the floor. "Dammit! I always drop things on the liny-oil-um."

Dandy can't seem to get her mouth around certain words, instantly turning into a three year old sounding things out for the first time.

"The what?" I tease.

"The lina, lina, loum.

I once read that, if in a dream you drop your food, it means that your body is trying to tell you to get rid of that food from your diet. I am about to tell Dandy that, but then I realize that the idea of giving up pizza would be as ridiculous as taking away her Yoo-Hoos. Those are her two basic food groups. So, I just go to my bedroom and get dressed.

"Are you picking up your *Whole Foods* hottie?" Dandy asks from the living room.

"No, we're meeting at the bar."

"Then what?" She asks.

"I don't know. Go out for pizza, I guess."

I'm mid-dressing as Dandy enters my bedroom. "You can't do that. She'll want something nicer."

"*You* never do." I tell her, as I pull up my pants.

"That's because I'm not sleeping with you."

"What does that have to do with it?"

"Because friends don't need to impress each other. We make no demands on one another. That's why it's so awesome."

"And that's why I can only have pizza with you?"

"You can have pizza with whomever you'd like. I'm just saying, just because *I* appreciate it, doesn't mean *she* will."

I'm fully dressed now. I kiss Dandy on the forehead as I exit. "I'll keep that in mind, my friend."

"Don't say I didn't warn you!"

As I walk down the boardwalk, I anticipate the next bit. Dandy's head sticking out above from my bedroom window. I look up at the window before she pops her head out.

"*Felix's* on Santa Monica! I'll be there tonight if..."

I wave her off. "Good night and good luck."

Chapter Eight

Dandy:

Other than visiting Simon at the bar, I never go to bars anymore. About a year ago, all the desire to hang out in loud places with a bunch of drunk people entirely left my system. Some people think this happens when we get older. I say it happens when we get wiser. I also don't like to stay out until three in the morning anymore. Some people think this happens when you get old. I say this happens because... okay, fine, I'm old and tired, and I get cranky in loud places. Whatever. I don't miss it. But back when I did frequent the clubs, *Felix's* was one of my go-to places. It was relaxed without being hipster. Classy without being snobby. Trendy without having to try too hard. That's why, when I walked past the velvet rope tonight and through the large, wrought iron double doors, I was kind of... blown away.

Wall to wall MEN. Hot, totally ripped, bare chested except for a bow tie, *MEN*. The loud, repetitive base of techno music pounded on. It would appear that Felix has come out of the closet.

I notice ex Kevin, looking as hot as ever. Actually, *hotter*. Also tanner and more ripped.

He's in the midst of singing, *I Will Survive.* Well, that answers that. I take out my notebook and cross out his name.

He notices me.

"Dandy? Is that you?"

I belly up to the bar. "Hey, Kevin. So, this place..."

"Switched ownership. Isn't it great?" Kevin beams.

"Grey Goose martini, please," I ask.

Kevin starts making my drink. I snag an olive from the garnish tray. "So, I guess a reconciliation is out of the question."

Kevin hands me my martini. "Dandy, I meant to tell you."

"You knew?" I ask.

"I had an inkling," he smiles.

I finish my drink in short order. "More please."

He gets to fixing another drink.

"You had an inkling?" I repeat.

"I had an inkling," he repeats.

"You had an inkling," I mutter again.

"Please don't do that thing you do," he says, handing me my drink.

"What thing do I do?"

"You repeat the last thing I say. You always do that."

"I always do that?"

"You just did."

"Nobody always does anything," I say. "It's a blanket statement wrapped up in overemphasis and an exaggeration based in a loose generalization."

Kevin smiles, pleased. *"You're in therapy? That's great!"*

"Yeah, isn't it?" I say, as I down my martini like it's just a cheap shot in pretty stemware.

Dammit. I swallowed an olive.

Chapter Nine

Simon:

My date, Sandra, is a pretty twenty-one year old, who flirted with me hard when we met. I kind of assumed she was into health, since I met her at *Whole Foods,* but she surprised me by not wanting dinner but just drinks at the bar. My bar. Not a prob, except, I'm sitting at the bar that I work at, while she dances on the dance floor with her girlfriends. I guess she told them to meet us here. Which is also kind of weird, but, no worries. I watch her dance. I've been doing that for about an hour now.

"Hey, Sandra! Do you wanna take a break for a sec?" I scream over the noise.

"What? Did you say something?" She screams back to me.

I join her on the dance floor, even though I don't dance in public. I sway my hips a bit. "Let's leave. I don't love being here on my night off. Maybe we can get a pizza or something?"

"Pizza!?" She yells at me, aghast. "Are you crazy? I haven't done dairy or carbs in three years! Hey, be a doll, and get me another." She thrusts her empty margarita glass into my hands.

"Sure." I take the glass and add, "then maybe we can go take a walk or something?"

"*Walk?*" Again, aghast. "Why would we do that? I have my car with me!"

"Right." I make my way to the bar with her empty glass. I think about telling her that there's sugar in the margarita mix, making it a carb-heavy cocktail choice, but I decide that I don't have energy to yell over the music again.

I feel a headache coming on as I make my way to my bar.

On my night off.

Chapter Ten

Dandy:

"But, you had sex with me! We had sex! *We had lots and lots of heterosexual... Sexual... Sex!*"

I may have had one too many. They should really be careful with over-serving at this place.

"Sweetheart," Kevin says in a hushed tone. "That was a very difficult time for me."

"Difficult? Having sex with me was difficult?" I start to cry. Drunk cry. I can tell he's trying not to laugh.

"No, I didn't mean it like that..."

"I'm a *girl,* Kevin!" I snap. "A gay boy can't sleep with a girl and still be gay! It's not allowed!" Still crying. Louder now.

A guy with a bullwhip passes by and interjects, "She has a point."

Kevin lashes out at the whip guy. Funny, you'd think it'd be the other way around. "Well, I'm no longer confused."

"He was confused," I tell Whip Guy.

Whip Guy gives us both a compassionate nod. "Fair enough," he shrugs and walks away.

After a moment I say, "Oh my God, does this mean that when you called me "girlfriend" you meant, *"guurlfriend?"*

I cry some more while Kevin comforts me. "Come on, Dand, it's going to be okay."

"You said you loved me," I whimper.

"I did. Just not in that way."

"Did I do this?" Did I make you gay?"

"Not exactly."

"What kind of answer is that? You can't make someone gay! That wasn't the right answer.

That wasn't the right answer at all!"

"What I meant was, you helped me see that I needed to be honest with myself."

"I did that?" I stop crying.

"Yes. *Your* self-obsession forced me to reexamine my *own* self-obsession, which in turn, allowed me to discover and claim my *true self.*"

"Really?"

"You were so ballsy and self-centered, you gave me the courage to be the same. Didn't you get my note?"

"Note? Oh, that's what you meant by *thank you*?" I say, picking up my head and wiping my eyes.

"Yes."

I look up at Kevin, and I search for his eyes, squinting through my tears and alcohol induced blur. He looks happy. He's calm, centered, in charge of his life. Did I have something to do with this new Kevin? The fact that I had even a smidgen of influence makes me feel proud. I actually helped someone see himself honestly without even trying. If only I could do the same for myself.

"Then... I guess... you're welcome."

I blow my nose into a cocktail napkin as Kevin and I forgive each other in silence.

Chapter Eleven

Dandy:

I'm rolling around the cafe with Debbie, telling her all about the night before. I tell her that I stumbled out of there with the conclusion that my self-obsession can be used for good and not evil.

"So, does this mean you're going to stop harassing your victims?" Debbie asks.

"No way. By the end of all of this I will have my entire, pathetic love life, all figured out."

Simon comes riding up on his retro bike. "How'd it go, Hot Lips?"

M.A.S.H. marathon on TV. We're oddly obsessed with TV shows that were on before we were born.

"Hey Simon, what's up?" Debbie greets Simon in their customary exchange.

"Hey, Deb." Simon nods.

Simon's phone gets a text ding. I look over his shoulder and notice it's from his ten-year-old niece, Ashley. They often meet up so he can give her advice about life. It's very sweet. My only family is my gramps, and I seem him regularly, too. He's a holocaust survivor, but he doesn't talk about it much. He's smart, funny and not afraid of anything. I look forward to my visits with gramps the way I imagine Simon looks forward to his visits with Ashley.

Simon texts Ashley back, then asks me, "So, Kevin was gay, right?"

"What? You knew?"

"I had a feeling."

"And you didn't think to tell me?"

Simon pulls on his ear. It's one of his quirks. He does it when he's nervous. "Well, it's not exactly something that's easily worked into conversation. Hey, Dandy, I like your hair cut, and, by the way, I think your boyfriend's playing for the other team."

A homeless guy passes by us and says, "Nice approach, pal."

"You see?" Simon says.

"You really like my hair cut?" I ask.

Simon shakes his head and rides away. "See you later."

I call after him. "Hey, how was *Whole Food's* girl?"

"Turns out she didn't want me to pick her up in case I was a party pooper."

"And?"

"Every party needs a pooper."

***

Later that night I find myself in my favorite old bookstore, *The Loft.* I don't have a Kindle, and I prefer holding a book in my hands and smelling the paper and putting it up on my shelf. I'm not sure if book-smelling is a common thing, but it should be. Books smell like black and white movies, fireplaces, and the past. Just being surrounded by all of these words, thoughts, ideas, discoveries, makes me dizzy with possibilities.

I'm sitting cross-legged in the aisle of the Psychology section. It's my IRL Web MD. The current book that is enjoying my adoration is the massive *DSM, Diagnostic and Statistical Manual of Mental Disorders.*

This book points out all of the delightful disorders I may possess. Such as Expressive Language Disorder, Mixed Receptive-Expressive Language Disorder, Communication Disorder, Conduct Disorder, Delirium and Delusions. Such a find! With this treasure I can self-diagnose all day long! I may currently be exhibiting signs of Social Phobia, Depressive Disorder, Obsessive-Compulsive Disorder, and Separation Anxiety Disorder! I remember having a Shih Tzu who had that last one.

A half-asleep clerk comes by to tell me I'm blocking the aisle. Tic disorder. Oh, I don't have that. I'm not sure. I ask the clerk, "I don't have a tic, do I?"

"You're creating a fire hazard," she tells me.

I apologize and stand up. I notice two, incredibly ripped guys across the aisle. The clerk notices, too, and she says, "Infatuation with homosexual men disorder. Page 47."

My left eye feels kind of twitchy.

Chapter Twelve

Simon:

Dandy is sitting at the bar eating cherries from my fruit tray. I remind her nightly that this bar is not her private buffet and that maraschino cherries are practically poison. But, in one ear and out the other.

She tells me between bites, "So, Jeremy will be a piece of cake. He was a nice guy. He made a fantastic red wine vinaigrette. A man who makes fantastic red wine vinaigrette can't possibly hold a grudge."

A guy comes up and orders two cosmos and a Diet Coke. I get the order together while Dandy watches on and continues, "You liked Jeremy, remember?"

"The fireman? Sure. Everybody likes firemen."

"Yeah, he was dreamy in that buff, heroic way."

"If Jeremy was so dreamy, why did you leave him?"

She practically does a spit take. *"I* left him?"

"Twenty-one," I tell my customer.

"Blackjack!" The customer laughs. I laugh along with him to keep his laughter company.

The guy proceeds to put exactly twenty-one dollars down on the bar, does a little 'tap-tap' on the bar and leaves with his drinks. I can't believe he stiffed me! He attempted a joke, I faked a laugh, and he still stiffs me!

As if she could read my thoughts Dandy says to the guy, "Excuse me, sir? You forgot to leave a tip."

I'm about to be mortified, but before I'm able to react, the guy comes back. Mumbling an apology, he puts a ten dollar bill on the bar and leaves.

Dandy smiles at me. "May this serve as a reminder, my friend. Sometimes in life, you just have to ask for what you want."

"Ask and I shall receivith?"

"*Askith* and you shall receivith. Yes."

"Will you please go now? You're distracting me from my work."

And with that... she leaves. She turns around as she exits. "See? How easy was that?"

Chapter Thirteen

Dandy:

I'm singing along to the oldies station. I'm in a pretty good mood, considering my last meeting ended with me sobbing my drunken eyes out at a gay bar.

"Hang on, Sloopy, Sloopy, Hang on. Jeremy lives in a very bad part of town ...

I sing into my iPhone recorder app. *"And everybody tries to put my Jeremy down. Jeremy, I don't care what I gotta do, 'cause you know Jeremy, boy, I'm gonna inter-view you... haaaang on Jere-my. Jere-my, hang on..."*

I pull into the fire station and spot him. Wow, he's still hot. Ha. Funny, being that he fights fires and all. I hit record. "Jeremy Phillips, 37, Northridge, California, Fire fighter, break up due to... me, I guess."

"Dandy? Is that you?" Jeremy says.

I get out of my car and approach him. "Live and in person." I open up my arms for a hug, not quite sure if an embrace is forthcoming or not. Luckily, it is.

"That's so weird, I just had a dream about you!" Jer-emy laughs, as he gives me a massive bear hug and swings me around in circles like I'm a paper doll. I forgot how strong he was. His pal, my former pal through him, Matt, notices.

"Hey, Dandy! How the heck are ya?" Matt asks.

Jeremy finally puts me down. "Hey, Matt."

"It's great to see you," Jeremy says.

Matt interjects, "Are you back to mend Jeremy's heart?"

"Don't jinx it man," Jeremy tells Matt. "Maybe she had a change of heart."

"Change of heart about what?" I ask. I really can't remember.

Just as I say that, an alarm goes off in the fire station. I'm guessing there's a fire somewhere, because everyone springs into action.

"Gotta run. Come over tonight, and I'll make your favorite. I perfected my baked ziti. You'll love it." Jeremy says as he rushes off.

But I'm on a mission, so, I follow him. "Actually, I just have a few questions…"

I catch up to him. "I'm doing a project..."

He hops up onto the fire truck, and for some reason, I feel like it's a good idea for me to do the same. So, I do. He looks at me with a kind of amazed look on his face, but he doesn't tell me to go away. So, I don't.

I scream over the siren. "I need to know why we broke up! I don't think it was something horrible, it's just that I can't put my finger on what it was exactly!" The truck is going breakneck speeds now. I've never gone breakneck speeds before. It's kind of awesome in a scary-pee-your-pants sort of way.

He smiles, leans in and yells, "That's because there was no good reason!"

We arrive at a home in flames. Wow. It's just like that movie, "Backdraft." And, for awhile, they had the "Backdraft" stop on the Universal Studios Tour, and I loved it. This is just like that! Except... really freakin' hot. Oh, and also, this is real. Jeremy puts on some sort of mask, and he hands me one. Matt rushes by, but first stops to place a helmet on my head. I continue interrogating Jeremy, as we make our way into the burning house. "I mean, did I say something? Did I do something? I tend to say and do things."

"We all say things, Dandy. We all do things."

"Yes. But... what exactly?"

I'm sure we are breaking all kind of rules here, me being a civilian and all, but I push that thought away, as I make sure to follow Jeremy closely through the smoke. As I step over a fallen burning beam, I imagine I'm starring in an action film with Tom Cruise. Then I wonder if I did a film with Tom Cruise if he would try to convert me to Scientology. Then they'd say that I can't speak with Simon anymore, because there's no way I could convince him to become a Scientologist. I wouldn't be able to convince gramps either, and he would yell at me in Yiddish, and maybe I would do a *Dateline* expose and become famous. Focus, Dandy, focus! Where was I? Oh, Jeremy, right.

"Didn't we used to go camping a lot? I remember hiking. We hiked. We had fun doing that, right?"

Jeremy fights the fire with sexy abandon. He yells back at me, "Maybe we had too much fun, and you got scared."

Just as he says that, the other fire fighters push through, another beam falls around me and this time I let out a huge scream. Jeremy sweeps me up after one of his pals screams, "GET HER OUT OF HERE!"

He carries me off to safety with one hand, while he holds a cute, grey kitten he saved in his other hand. Standing outside of the house, out of breath, full of soot, I ask him, between coughs, "So… (cough, cough) are you saying (cough cough) I was (cough cough) afraid?"

"I'm saying, I asked you to marry me, and you vanished into thin air. I'm saying that I told you that I wanted a family, and you started to hyperventilate."

In that moment, it all came back to me. He was a major family guy, and he wanted… *ten children.*

"You wanted ten children!" I yell.

"My mom and dad had ten children. What's wrong with a large family?"

"Nothing, If you're *Octomom.* Besides, don't you know that the world is totally overpopulated, and in the future we won't even have enough food for all the people on the planet if we keep procreating the way we are?"

"You don't want a family?"

"Not ten children! What about my career?"

"You don't have a career."

"Not with ten children I don't!"

"You can't have everything, Dandy." He says too sweetly for me to hate him.

"Who says?"

We stare at one another for what feels like a year and a half. Maybe I *could* change. Maybe I *should* change. He seems to still be into me.

A beautiful woman with some sort of slutty accent approaches. She says to Jeremy, "You saved my Pookie!" She takes the kitten from Jeremy and pushes it into her breasts. Okay, she was probably aiming for her heart.

Jeremy removes his gaze from me, and BAM, just like that. He's smitten with the girl and her pussy. Cat.

"Yes, I did save your Pookie." He smiles at her. Now Jeremy and the foreign temptress have their eyes locked. She thanks him profusely, as he continues to say things like, "Just doing my job, Miss."

"So... I'll be in the truck." I inform him.

As I pout in the fire truck, I watch the new love-birds make googly-eyes at one another. Then I take out my notebook and firmly cross Jeremy's name off the list.

Chapter Fourteen

Grandpa Joe:

She is a funny, little pisher, that Dandy. It would appear she is in some sort of… how you say… a pickle? We drive in my new lawnmower. Oy, it's a beautiful thing! Such a lawnmower you never did see! It is a John Deere X758. They tell me it is the Rolls-Royce of lawnmowers. I work hard all my life. I deserve a little extra treat, no? I call my new lawnmower *Dolores*, after my late wife, may she rest in peace. What would my Dolores think of me naming a lawnmower after her? She would laugh and smile at me with her eyes dancing, and she would tell me I am a crazy-old man. In other words, she would have loved it. I give Dandy a pair of safety goggles, and off we go to mow. Mowing the lawn on my Dolores is the thing I most love to do. Now Dandy begins to do the thing she most loves to do... the yakety yak.

"The thing is, if I *know* that I have an *Acute Narcissism Disorder* or serious *Delusions of Grandeur* then that's the first step to recovery!"

I don't know what she's talking about. She reads too much, thinks too much, talks to much, wonders too much. But, what can you do? When you love someone, you listen, no? I turn to my lovely granddaughter, and I ask her, "So, did you and that Simon ever smooch a little?"

"What?"

"Well, I'm just saying, it makes the sense, no?"

"No, it does not make the sense. I'm trying to tell you that I'm on the verge of solving all of my love problems, and you want to know if I've kissed my best friend?"

"Boobila, it is not so crazy."

"Yes. It is. Besides you, Simon is the only man I can't turn into a nut job."

"My, my, my, you certainly think you have a lot of power, don't you?"

"You've seen what happens, gramps. I make them cuckoo, and then they leave. All of them. First it was dad, then it was every man I ever dated. Either that or *I* do the leaving before they can, in order to beat them to the punch. Either way, I end up alone."

"Let me ask you, in your psychiatric mumbo jumbo, it is okay to give yourself a lot of these silly labels and make everything so complicated?" I ask.

"Labels can help us stay organized. They're one way to try and understand each other and ourselves better. At least I think that. Or I *think* I think that."

Then she does something that is nothing short of miraculous. My darling granddaughter *stops talking*. So, I take advantage of this opening. "Your grandma and me, we never needed to put such labels all over each other. We knew each other just the right amount. And if one of us should sometimes act a little cuckoo, we forgave each other."

Dandy is still not talking as we drive along on Dolores. I notice her watching the blades of grass pop up from under Dolores. She has a look on her face like she is missing something, somebody. I know the look too well.

"Listen," I tell her. "When you meet someone whose cuckoo matches your cuckoo in all of the right ways, it will be a match. So far, these boys happen to be not the right kind of cuckoo for you. In the meantime, boobila, quiet your mind a little, yes?"

She looks at me and almost says something but instead, she smiles. I know she's not going to make me any promises she can't keep.

Chapter Fifteen

Dandy:

There's another dream I have about once a year. I have no memory of my dad, so I have no way of knowing if he and my mom were ever happy together. I do have one photo of him, though. He's leaning against a red Jeep, smiling into the camera with a grin on his face, like he just got away with something, and wouldn't you like to know what? He has the butt end of a lit cigarette dangling from his lips. He's wearing a striped brown derby hat. He has bushy eyebrows, but even so, he was without argument a very good-looking man. He looks like he could charm the pants off of you. Which I guess is exactly what he did to my mom, who had me about 9 months after meeting him.

My mom was there too. She was stunningly beautiful and serene, with blonde, wavy hair and big, blue knowing eyes. I remember she was always laughing. Not the kind of laugh you laugh after hearing a joke but the kind of laugh where you are so full of joy that you have no choice but to laugh.

My mom and dad are sailing on the clear, blue ocean, over calm waters, the wind in their hair, they hold on to one another tightly. Mom was joyous, and dad was charming. And together, in this yearly dream of mine, they were deeply, undeniably in love. It's as if nothing outside of themselves on that sailboat on that perfect summer day could harm them.

Then the sea gets suddenly choppy and huge, ten foot swells begin to rock them violently around the boat. They lose their balance. My dad lets go of my mom to tend to the boat, and my mom's smile starts to fade as she watches him go. He looks like he's about to take the helm, but instead he tips his hat to my mom and *dives off the ship,* leaving mom alone on the rocking boat. Then there's a baby's cry heard from inside the cabin. I can't see they baby, but I'm guessing *I'm* that baby. My mom's smile returns briefly. But not completely. The baby's cries get louder and louder, and mom slowly begins to vanish. First it's her left arm, then her right, then her legs. A piece of her keeps vanishing one at a time, as the baby's cries grow louder, the wind whips the boat to and fro until finally... mom is completely gone. The baby is now alone on the rocking boat in the middle of the storm. Still crying.

That's when I wake up. Disappointed that the dream always ends the same way.

Everything was perfect until dad jumped ship and mom disappeared.

I feel painfully sad for that baby.

***

I'm at the café day-dreaming. I don't know how people do it, but they do. Maybe not for a long time and maybe not in an ideal way but people, all the time, are hooking up and staying hooked up for awhile. And during that time, they get to be in that world I so enjoy and miss. Coupledom.

"Miss? Excuse me? Anyone home?"

I snap out of my daydream to wait on a couple. It occurs to me that maybe I should start asking actual *couples* how they do it instead of interrogating my exes. Or at least in addition to interrogating my exes.

"One veggie sandwich on sourdough, hold the mayo, hold the oil, hold the salt and a strawberry daiquiri," I repeat back to my first customer of the day.

"Yes," she confirms.

"One roast beef on white, extra everything and scotch on the rocks," I repeat back to her boy-friend/date/husband/fiancé/whatever.

"Yes," he confirms.

They could not possibly have more opposing taste in food. I wonder if it's like that with everything. "Can I ask you something?"

"Sure."

"What kind of music do you like?"

"Classical."

"And you?" I ask the woman.

"Speed metal."

I continue, directing my next question back at the guy, "Favorite movie?"

"Little Women."

"Really?" I respond. He nods and I ask the same question to the woman.

"Boogie Nights."

They don't seem to mind my questions, so I continue. Back to the man, "Religious affiliation?"

"Conservative Jew," he says.

"Pagan," she says.

I can take no more. "Good luck to you both." I walk away with less answers than I started out with.

I find Deb and follow her around as she serves her tables. "So, you see, we are all doomed. All of us. Nobody makes any sense together, and if they do, they have no idea *why* they do, so they can be of no help to others. The whole thing is futile."

Debbie places the food down in front of her customers. "Stop being so dramatic." She turns to her customers and says, "You two seem happy. How long have you been married?"

"We're not married," says the guy.

"Oh," Debbie says. "I saw the rings and assumed they were wedding bands."

"They are," says the woman.

"We *are* married," adds the guy.

"Just not to each other," whispers the woman.

Debbie walks away and turns to me. "We are all doomed."

We make our way to the kitchen, and I can't seem to stop my rambling, "Relationships are impossible, how can you expect two people, from totally different homes, different upbringings, different ideas about the world, about themselves, how can we ever make it with anyone?"

Angelo, the pudgy, older Italian chef interjects in his thick Italian accent, "Who you want to make it with, Dandolino?"

"No, Angelo. I don't want to "make-it" with anyone," I tell him.

Debbie flirts with Angelo. "Make it?" Who says that? How old is that expression anyway?"

Angelo smiles. "It's a timeless expression, amore mio, just like your beauty."

"Interesting," Debbie coos. "Keep talking."

I lost her. When Debbie gets caught up in flirtsville, she's a goner for awhile. I swear, this girl takes flirting to a whole new level. She once made the new busboy, Orlando, have an actual heart attack and trip over a table and drop a bucket of dirty dishes, because she held a smile too long in his general direction. Turned out he had a major heart condition, but still, Debbie's got mad flirting skills.

"I love Italians," she mouths to me.

I hope Angelo has a strong heart.

Chapter Sixteen

Simon:

I woke up on the wrong side of the bed. Actually, it's just the opposite of that. I woke up on the *same* side of the bed that I always wake up on. I had my cup of coffee out of the *same* mug I always have my coffee out of. Now I'm walking down the *same* boardwalk to my *same* job. I will see the *same* people I see every day. Is this how other people do life?

I like things mellow, yes, but there is such a thing as too mellow. Too… *samey.* Everything I do, I've done before. I thought it would be different by this point in my life. By thirty-five, I figured I'd have a career that I love, not just a job that I tolerate. I'd have a wife and maybe one or two little ones running about. My wife and I would have a few couple-friends we'd have over for dinner on the weekends. A *real* dinner, with fresh vegetables and maybe a fancy French dessert. A dessert that didn't come prepackaged from Hostess. But that's not what I got. What I got is the carefree life of a twenty-five-year-old. Without the carefree part.

Because I worry. I worry like a man who is fast approaching midlife who has yet to start a life. People think men don't worry about this stuff, and maybe some don't, but I do. I need to do something, because what I have here is a life with no surprises. I've painted myself into a corner of safe, and now I'm trapped in that corner and I'm restless.

I'm a writer, so why don't I spend my days writing? I even had one moment of success as a writer. I wrote a short story that was published in a local Venice paper. It was called, *Keep it Rollin'*. It was about a guy who was in love with a girl but was too afraid to tell her, so instead he just kept on rollin' through the friendship without ever telling her.

Man, I'm beginning to really get on my own nerves.

I'm skating down the boardwalk to clear my head. The salt air sometimes momentarily wakes me up when I feel like I'm sleepwalking through my life. Harry Perry has been playing his guitar and skating behind me for about ten minutes now.

"Hey! Wait up!" Dandy yells.

She's coming up fast on her white, old-school skates, not blades. She's smiling broadly, the way that she does. I don't slow down.

"Hey! Slow down!" She yells again, this time catching up to me.

"Where are you off to?" She asks as she squeezes past Harry Perry.

"Nowhere. I'm going absolutely nowhere," I tell her.

"Oh, you're having one of those days." She nods sympathetically.

"I'm just tired of not doing anything."

"You do stuff," Dandy insists. "You write! You're an awesome writer."

"I haven't written anything in months. What I am is a bartender. That's it. I'm just a bartender."

"You are not *just* a bartender. That's like saying I'm *just* a waitress."

"Well, aren't you?"

Dandy stops skating, making Harry ram right into her. She takes out a bill and hands it to Harry. "We're having a little crisis, Harry. Do you mind?"

Harry takes the cash and skates away, still singing.

Dandy looks at me seriously. "Neither of us are *just* anything. People are more than their jobs."

We skate off to a bench and sit down. "Then what are we?" I ask.

A bunch of the local homeless guys have started a drum circle of sorts near us. The pounding is comforting. These cats got rhythm but where did they get the drums?

"We're just humans. Human people. Just… living our lives, trying to figure things out. That's all." She tells me as she bops her head to the sounds of the drums.

"We're floaters." I tell her as I gaze out into the ocean. The vast ocean makes me think of the vastness of time. There's so much of it. So much behind us, hopefully a lot in front of us. People are always saying how there isn't enough time. How there isn't enough space. It doesn't feel like that when you stare into the ocean and you're just… being. I just wish I was being something specific.

"Just because we haven't figured out our entire lives yet does not make us floaters."

"Slackers?"

"We have jobs. We're not slackers."

"Losers?"

Dandy starts to pace-skate, which is really just skating in a figure eight. She does this, because she can't sit still. She's always been like that. Once, in the seventh grade, she changed seats five times at lunch. She probably had ADD, but kids weren't diagnosed and drugged as much back then. Well, they were drugged, but usually that was their own doing.

"We have a life, Simon!" she rants. "We're not float-ers, losers, slackers, wanderers, or any other *er* word!"

Dandy tends to find "projects" to busy herself with. Maybe that keeps her busy enough where she can actually trick herself into thinking that she's living a full life.

I tell her, "We work. We eat pizza. We skate on the boardwalk. You even yell at Harry Perry everyday. It's all so… rut-like."

She sits back down and says, "Maybe this is what our lives look like. Not everybody has to have big plans and colorful lives. There's nothing wrong with where we are. Besides, I'm currently in the process of discovery. You'd feel better if you got yourself a project, like mine."

But I know that tracking down my "significant" ex-girlfriend would be a depressing and not terribly time-consuming feat. If for anything else, because there's no "s" at the end of girlfriend.

Dandy interrupts my thoughts. "Do you ever hear from Julia?"

Julia is my ex. She was a lot of work. She was too suspicious. Like, she could never get over why I was such close friends with Dandy. She always said, "Why do you need her?" As if Dandy were a drug or something.

Dandy watches me, waiting for an answer, and trips over the same curb she always trips over. She falls to the ground. The same ground.

"Dammit! Who put that there?" She exclaims, looking up.

I help her up and remind her, "You always trip over that curb."

As I help her up, she falls into me and into a hug of sorts. Our eyes meet. It was a mistake and kind of awkward. I mean, it's not like we've never hugged before, but this somehow feels… different. We are both silent for a second, looking at each other. Her eyes are as green as jade. Behind them is a type of wonder and a playfulness that's spontaneous and brave, and now I'm wondering if I ever noticed that before.

"Simon?" she whispers.

"Yeah?" I say.

"Let's play hooky tonight and go to the Getty!" She's skating around now, excited.

"I have to work." I remind her.

"Yeah, well, you said we're in a rut. So, let's do something un-rutty. Come on! My treat!"

"The museum is free," I tell her. Which is kind of strange, since I read that J. Paul Getty was a penny pincher. You'd think he'd charge a fortune to visit his place. Maybe he was just cheap when he was alive, so he could afford to not charge us admission when he was dead. So, in a way, he was cheap for us. In which case, we owe it to him to visit his museum.

"Fine," I agree.

"Fine! He said fine! Whooo-hooo!" She yells to no one in particular as she skates away and proceeds to trip over the same curb again, except this time she doesn't fall to the ground.

"You see? It's all good, Simon. All good."

Chapter Seventeen

Dandy:

I don't understand French "m" words. I mean, when we say Merlot, we don't pronounce the "t." When we say Moet we do pronounce the "t." Then there's Monet. What do we do? How are we expected to just know these things? I'm thinking lofty thoughts such as these as Simon and I walk around the Getty.

Simon is still in a funk. I hate it when he gets like this. He seems so sad and distant. Sometimes it's a fulltime job trying to cheer him up. But I'm good at it. Getting a laugh out of Simon always makes me feel like I won the lottery on the eighth night of Hanukah.

But Hanukah presents were never that great, so I like to think I also won the lottery on that night. Anyhow, Simon's a tough nut to crack, but I've made it a game to play the nutcracker.

"Why did you break up with Julia?" I ask him, trying to shock him out of his funk. "Because of dreams."

"Dreams, like goals? Or dreams like the nighttime stories in our head?"

"Nighttime. She didn't believe in them. She thought that everyone made up those stories in order to have something interesting to talk about."

"But isn't there, like, proof that we dream?"

"That's exactly what I told her, but she didn't buy it." He shrugs.

Apparently Julia thinks that when we close our eyes, there's complete and total darkness, and that's it. It's just one person's opinion about one thing, so why did it bother Simon enough for him to break up with her? I know why. Because Simon hates it when people shut their minds up super closed with an idea and they don't consider other possibilities.

Also, he prefers stories rather than darkness.

We reached Monet's *La Promenade* painting. It's a painting of a woman with an umbrella in a field with a small boy. It looks like the wind is blowing. The woman glances black at us, surprised, with a hint of sadness in her face. It's beautiful. I don't know why it's beautiful or what it means, or what Monet was thinking when he painted it. I just know how it makes me feel. It makes me feel like there's hope and peace and beauty in the world.

And for that, I love this painting.

"Hey, what was that Monet quote on that poster? Remember, the one that hung in that coffee house in the valley we used to go to?" Simon asks me, not taking his eyes off the painting.

"Can't remember." I shrug.

We continue looking at the painting as if we are waiting for it to change. Maybe it does change. Not in the way those paintings at the Haunted Mansion in Disneyland change, but in a subtle, mysterious way. Of course paintings don't change.

We only change how we look at them.

I feel Simon staring at me. I look at him, and he quickly looks away. Huh, that's weird. I watch Simon's face as he continues to enjoy the painting. He has such a strong nose. I don't mean that to mean big; I mean that to mean strong. Manly. I'm not sure why I never noticed his nose before, but it really is a good, strong, manly nose. And he has great skin. How does he get it to look so good? He must moisturize. Yeah, I'll bet he moisturizes. Plus he always has a great tan from all that skating on the boardwalk.

Simon must have felt my stare, because he turns to me. I quickly look away. Staring at someone is rude. And embarrassing. I must not let that happen again.

He's still looking at me. I can feel it.

I quickly walk away from the painting. "I think I've seen everything."

Chapter Eighteen

Simon:

My karate gi doesn't fit perfectly, but I'm making it work. *KI-AH!* I enjoy karate chopping the air. I got all the way to blue belt when I was in the seventh grade. I kept the karate gi, but not the karate flare, which, if I'm being totally honest, I never had to begin with. I have a little steam to let out so I'm getting my *karate on* while I watch late-night television in my own apartment tonight. I spend too much time with Dandy. I feel I should give her some space. Plus, I think she caught me staring at her at the museum earlier, and that's just weird, because friends aren't supposed to stare at their friends' faces.

KI-AH!

Besides, a little "me time" isn't so bad. Everyone's always talking about how important it is and everything, so I might as well experience some of it myself.

I'm enjoying a late night infomercial in all its absurdity. I'm watching the backside of a studly looking guy demonstrating the amazingness of the *Butt Maestro* (patent pending.) The camera is tight on his tight bum, while the ridiculous host in the blindingly bright-orange wife-beater enthusiastically looks straight into the camera and says way too loudly, *"If this isn't the best butt cruncher you've ever tried, you will get a full refund, no questions asked!"*

Then the butt speaks. "I'm the tightest tush this side of the Mississippi river!"

I bust up laughing, as there are few things in life that are as joyful as a talking butt infomercial. I turn to laugh about it with Dandy but remember that she's not there. Now the camera pans up and closes in on the face of the butt owner. The guy looks familiar. At that moment, I hear Dandy's double knock on our shared wall, which is our code that means she's about to call, so I need to make sure I pick up.

Knock-knock. Ring-ring.

I pick up the phone. "Oh my God, that's Bobby! He's on the list!" she screams.

"The Butt Maestro (patent pending) Guy?"

"Yes!"

"Bobby is the butt?"

"Yes, Bobby is the butt!"

"I thought he looked familiar. I mean, his face. You know, he's still acting, so he should be easily IMDB."

"Yeah. He looks good, right?"

"I guess."

After a moment she says to me, "You're not wearing your gi again, are you?"

I look down, and I notice that my pants come up past my knees. But the belt fits just fine. "No, of course not," I tell her, as I tug my ear.

"Oh. I thought I heard KI-AHing."

"Nope. No KI-AHing here."

"I'm going to order a Butt Maestro (patent pending). Do you want one?" She asks.

"No, I'll just borrow yours."

We hang up, and she's off to find yet another ex, so she can discover further useless information about herself. And I will support her through it like I always do. Unless I don't. I mean, maybe I should just get busy doing my own thing, you know? Why do I always have to go along with Dandy's "things?"

KI-AH!

Chapter Nineteen

Debbie:

Another gorge day at the beach! So sunny and busy. It'll be a good tip day at the café. Because the day is hot, and I'm wearing my halter-top bathing suit, the "miracle suit" one that sucks in the bad stuff and pushes up the good stuff. You know the one I'm talking about. It's hot. I'm hot. It's gonna be a good day.

I'm thinking about all of this, while Dandy tells me the story of her recent life issues, while we both fill up the saltshakers before the breakfast crowd rushes in. She's complaining about Simon again. I swear, sometimes I have to tune that girl out, because she can be so damn repetitive. I love her and all, but how dense can a girl be? She should just jump Simon.

At least give it a whirl to alleviate all of this tension.

I tell her this a few times a week. "Just get it over with. Get him drunk to loosen him up. It's so simple. I never understood the two of you."

"I can't. We're just friends."

"Everybody is *just* something before they're just something else."

"You don't get it."

"What don't I get? You guys *act* like a couple. You *look* like a couple. So… you're a duck."

"What?"

"If it looks like a duck and it quacks like a duck, then it's a duck. So you and Simon, you guys are absolutely ducks."

"It would ruin everything."

"Maybe it'll make everything better."

"I don't want to lose him."

Ugh, it's like going around and around in a circle with this one. "You don't want to lose him so you'll never have him to begin with?"

"Yes. That's right. We're like family."

"Husband and wife is family."

"Whoa, husband and wife? You, of all people, are suggesting a committed, monogamous type of relationship between two people? That's not like you."

"People change."

"People do. But you don't." Dandy quips as she passes me an empty saltshaker. "I ran out of salt."

I fill the last shaker for her. "I happen to think that marriage is really a good thing. It's just the divorce part that I think is crummy."

"You do know that divorce is not actually *part* of marriage. It's not mandatory.

Yeah, right. Dandy knows the truth as well as I do, because both of our dads left when we were just kids. We didn't have an example of two happy parental units sharing a life "till death do they part." People just don't stay together. And I don't blame them. It's tough as shit to play nice with others. Compromising, staying interested, *listening.* That's a lot of work.

"Name two couples you know who are still together." I challenge her.

Dandy thinks for a second. "Okay… wait, why two? Why can't I just name one?"

"Fine, name one."

"Mr. Stuczynski who owns the bike repair shop on Main. He and Mrs. Stuczynski have been married for forty years!"

"Mrs. Stuczynski has been in a mental institution for twenty of those years."

"Yeah, but he visits her every other Sunday!"

"Find one couple, *living under the same roof,* that you can honestly say will most likely be together for the long haul."

Dandy's thinking so hard, I'm afraid she's going to give herself a stress migraine. I almost want to tell her to forget the whole thing, but part of me hopes she can think of a happy couple.

Dandy mumbles something like, "This is a stupid game," and skates off for the kitchen.

I think about following her, but then Chuck, one of our breakfast customers, arrives, wearing an ear-to-ear smile once he gets an eyeful of my miracle suit halter-top.

His tips are often larger than the bill itself.

Yes, it's gonna be a good day.

Chapter Twenty

Simon:

Do you ever feel like you're trapped in the movie *Groundhog Day?* You know the one where Bill Murray keeps repeating the same day over and over again? I'm doing that, but it's not nearly as fun or as funny as it was in the movie. I'm sitting on a bench on the boardwalk wondering what I should do. *What should I do with my life?* is such a big question, so, at this point, I would settle for, *What should I do with the rest of my day?* Or night. The nights are the worse. They feel so long and quiet, unless I'm with Dandy, and then they're usually fun and loud, but… but then there's that *Groundhog Day* again.

"Simon, what's up?" Debbie says, startling me out of my thoughts.

"Oh, hey, Debbie."

She sits down on the bench beside me. Too close. Too close is her way.

"You workin' tonight?" Debbie asks.

"No, not tonight. Probably just watching a movie with Dandy or something."

"Not tonight you're not. She has a date with Bobby, the butt." Debbie informs me.

"Oh?" I say, trying not to sound disappointed. "Cool." I add for good measure.

Debbie's eyes light up like she just had the most fantastic idea ever. Which somehow frightens me. This is already the longest conversation we've ever had without Dandy present.

"Hey!" she begins, "why don't you come with me to *Medieval Times* tonight? I have free tickets."

Medieval Times is a place where wars are acted out on horseback and people eat huge chicken legs with their hands. It's not the ideal locale for a sensitive brooder like myself.

"It's super fun!" exclaims Debbie.

Fun, unless you happen to be a vegetarian or a pacifist. And I happen to be both. "Yeah, I don't know. It's not really my thing."

"What is your thing?"

"I'm not sure yet. But I don't think it's *Medieval Times*."

"Can't know if you don't try." She tells me in a flirty tone she's never used on me before. I'm a bit flattered and a bit flustered. She must have noticed that and liked it, because her next move was a total power move. She grabbed my face in her hands and whispered, "I always thought we should get to know each other better." Really? She did? She never seemed to so much as notice me before. No, I can't be alone with Debbie. Dandy has told me stories about her. She always gets her way and can be quite manipulative. Besides, this is Dandy's best friend, and she might not like me hanging out with her alone and I don't trust Debbie so, no, no, the answer is no, absolutely no way am I going anywhere with this aggressive seductress. This could upset the whole order of things. Not the time-space continuum thing but my life thing. This can only mean trouble.

I'm going home STAT!

***

So here I am with Debbie at *Medieval Times* watching her devour her chicken leg while I eat tiny granules of rice with my fingers. She is going at that chicken leg like… well, I'm a vegetarian, so part of me thinks it's gross, the way she is enthusiastically holding it, worshipping it, enjoying it, and the other part of me is a man, so, yeah, it's really fucking hot.

"Isn't this awesome?!" She screams, slightly buzzed, eagerly watching the men in armor do their heroic play acting. "I love armor! Blue team will win. The blue team always wins."

"Do you come here a lot?" I ask her.

"Oh, yeah. War is sexy," she coos as she ruffles my hair.

This ruffling of the hair catches me by surprise and momentarily turns me into mush, so I proceed to accidentally spill the entire contents of my beer onto her shoes. "Oh! I'm sorry!"

I quickly try to clean it up with the one napkin I have.

"Don't worry about it." She doesn't seem terribly concerned, as she is still focused on the jousting. "I never liked these shoes."

"Really? These are great shoes. Dandy has a pair in red," I tell her.

Debbie stops watching the game, sits down and places her hands lightly upon my lap.

"You know what kind of shoes Dandy wears?" She places one hand to her heart. This is the first time I've ever seen this sweet, loving expression on Debbie's face. It's kind of weird.

She stares at me for awhile. It would appear that she is momentarily unconcerned about the chicken leg, the war, or her sticky beer shoes.

Dandy:

Bobby hasn't stopped talking for about an hour now. About himself. I almost stop him a few times to lightly suggest that maybe he'd like to try not being such an actor cliché, but he seems so happy, I don't have the heart. Besides, I'm so impressed that he took me to this fancy place for dinner, I'm in a quasi-shock. When we dated he was a strictly fast-food guy one hundred percent of the time. The first three drawers in his tiny apartment kitchen were packed full of those little packets. He had enough ketchup, hot sauce, mustard, mayo and relish to survive a famine. At least I think that stuff would keep you alive for a bit. You'd be disgustingly full of sodium and food dye color number 7, but alive.

"The movie went straight to video, but that's okay, because less people will see it that way, and that's good because I don't want to suffer from over-exposure. My agents are very concerned about that," he tells me.

I realize that now is a good time to speak, because there's an opening, but I'm not sure if I have enough time to add anything longer than a single word reply. I can seize this moment while he sips his wine… nope, too late, he grins at me, "You look good, Dand. Real good."

Bobby is a good looking guy, charming in that "self aware" sort of way, but still, when he compliments me, it gives me moths rather than butterflies. There's something about a man who's too self assured that creeps me out.

"Oh, thanks. So, this place is quite a step-up from Taco Bell," I add.

"Yeah, The Butt Maestro (patent pending) has been a godsend. I have... back end." He cracks himself up. "Get it? *Back end.*"

I watch Bobby laugh at his own joke for a bit, while I take the opportunity to refill my glass of wine.

Debbie:

I finally convinced Simon to put on the plastic crown. He's kind of cute in a sweet, quiet sort of way. Not usually my thing, though. I prefer cock-sure men who ooze confidence. I haven't been with a straight-up-nice-guy, like... ever. Dandy clearly doesn't want him, and he's too timid to make a move, so maybe I should step in and shake things up. For my sake and maybe their sake. I know, I know, it sounds so bad but is it really? I mean, life is for the living, right? I offer him some of my chicken leg, "Wanna bite?"

"I'm a vegetarian, remember?" He says as he gently pushes the chicken leg away.

"Oh, right. Just like Dandy," I remember. "Well, they didn't make many of you back then," I say, pointing at the jousters.

"Obviously," Simon agrees as rice slips through his fingers while he eats. Or tries to eat. Poor thing. He's probably hungry. Jeez, would it have killed them to throw a carrot into the mix?

The wizard is up! I stand up, excited. "The Wizard! I love this part! *SHHHH!*"

"I didn't say anything."

I love it when The Wizard rides in on his white horse. He speaks all dramatically about the evil black knight that he must fight. A cloud of smoke surrounding him. It's so sexy. The idea of a man, on a white horse, rushing in to save the day. To save me, from … from what exactly? From myself? I glance over at Simon. I could have him. Maybe not forever but for the night. But I shouldn't. But, he is technically available and so am I, so, why not?

"You and Dandy sure have a lot in common, huh?" I ask him casually, keeping my eyes on the Wizard the whole time.

"Yeah."

"It's too bad you two can't get together."

"What you mean?"

"It's a shame that you can't be a real couple."

"Well, I don't think it's that we *can't,* we just… choose not to."

The Wizard screams, "To Victory!" This is when everyone in the audience stands up and screams it back, "To Victory!" I nudge Simon to join in. He's late and unenthused, but he joins in. "Victory, yay."

"…And why is that?" I continue, "about you and Dandy?"

"Because, we're friends."

"Yeah, you wouldn't want to be friends with the person you're in love with. That would suck."

"She tells me I'm like a brother to her."

"Oh. Well, that's no good."

A man falls of his horse. Unexpected! Exciting! I stand up and cheer.

I'm the only one cheering, but I don't care.

Dandy:

I haven't had a chance to ask babbling Bobby a question yet. I swear, he could be a ventriloquist, he's so good at drinking, eating and talking at the same time. He pauses only to survey me, and in those moments, I'm too uncomfortable to speak. Like now. He's quiet for a second, and then he breaks his own silence with, "You really missed me, huh?"

"What? Excuse me?"

"You told me on the phone about your 'project,' but you don't have to make up some lame excuse to see me. I'm always here for you, babe."

"I didn't make anything up. I just have a few questions…"

"Listen, I know the hold I have on women. Most find me … irresistible. More wine?"

I try not to roll my eyes, as I flip open my notebook and jump right in. "Did you think I was... too needy? Not needy enough? Too dependent? Codependent? Overly optimistic? Selfish? Not willing to commit? Afraid of being abandoned? Moody? Removed? . . ."

Bobby interrupts me, "Whoa, hold it, there, tiger. I'm not sure I was paying all that much attention at the time. I just thought you were hot."

That's it? He didn't give our relationship much thought? He has no answers or thoughts of any kind on the subject? *He wasn't paying attention.* I'm flattered by the hot remark and annoyed by everything else.

Flattered and annoyed. I am feeling flatnoyed by babbling Bobby and his stupid talking butt.

Simon:

Why is Debbie suddenly so interested in my friend-ship with Dandy? I ask her, "Did Dandy set you up to this?"

"She doesn't even know we're out tonight," Debbie tell me. "She probably wouldn't like it very much if she did."

"Why would she care?"

"Open up your eyes, Simon. The bluebird of happiness, man."

I don't know what she's talking about. I rarely know what she's talking about. I stare at her blankly.

She continues, "Didn't you see the movie? You know, with that cute little girl with curly blonde hair, from the thirties or something, what's her name?"

"Shirley Temple?"

"Yeah! That's it!"

The Wizard screams, *To Victory*! This time I know what to do, so I stand up, along with everyone and yell, "To Victory!" Then I sit down to continue the conversa-tion, "What about Shirley Temple?"

Debbie says, "In her movie, *The Bluebird,* she was this poor girl who, through some kind of magic or some-thing, traveled with her little brother, and her dog and her cat, all around the place searching for the bluebird of happiness. They went into the past and couldn't find it, they even went to heaven and couldn't find it. They looked everywhere, absolutely everywhere." Debbie pauses, perhaps for effect.

"So?" I ask her, "Where was it?"

Debbie grins wildly, "It was in her backyard the whole time!"

Debbie sits down and puts her arm around my shoulder. She whispers in my ear,

"Don't be a dufus your whole life, Simon."

And then… Debbie, my friend-by-association for the past six years, pulls me close to her and… kisses me.

Dandy:

I think about leaving the restaurant, but Bobby now has theories he apparently wants to share with me; none of them, I suspect, will be terribly mind-blowing.

"I think it just… wasn't meant to be," he tells me.

This surprises me. This kind of new-agey spiritual talk is normal coming from me but not from this guy. "You believe in *meant to be*?"

"Not really," he admits, "but I might play a character one day who does believe in it, so I figured I'd try it on for size. It's pretty lame, though." Bobby laughs.

"I can't believe this. It's as simple as Simon said it was," I mumble.

"*Simon says.* That's funny! Hey, is that the same Simon you've been tight with all this time?"

"Yup."

"You two haven't hooked up yet?"

"No."

"Huh." He says as he has another gulp of wine. He winks at me and says, "So, are we gonna do it tonight or what?"

I take out my notebook and cross off Bobby's name right in front of him. It's okay, he's checking out his own face in the reflection of the spoon now, so he didn't notice.

Simon:

I didn't ask for that kiss from Debbie, but I didn't exactly pull away either. She *is* really pretty, and I've known her a long time… no, no, stop it, Simon, don't just jump into something, because you're feeling lonely, and because a hot chick is throwing herself at you. Be a man. But, wait, wouldn't a *man* jump on this?

"You seem worried," Debbie notices.

"Um… why did you kiss me?"

"Our team is winning. Plus, I like you."

"You do?"

"Do you want me to come over tonight?"

"No! Absolutely not!" I say too strongly.

"Gee, thanks," she says, hurt. Or mock-hurt. I can't tell.

I didn't mean to be such a dick about it. This is Dandy's best friend. Isn't there some sort of code where we don't mess around with friends of friends without written notice or verbal approval first or something?

"Don't you like me?" Debbie pouts.

"Of course I do, I just… I don't think it's a good idea."

She starts kissing my neck and nibbling on my ear, slowly, sensually.

The Wizard yells, "To Victory!" But this time we don't get up.

Debbie whispers in my ear, "It's okay. You can think of someone else."

PART TWO

Chapter Twenty-One

Dandy:

I've been standing in front of the fridge long enough to need a sweater. I think about going and getting a sweater but figure it would be easier to just grab something, anything, out of the fridge and then shut the fridge door. I grab a Yoo-Hoo and shut the fridge door. I hear sounds from Simon's apartment. It sounds like he has a guest over. He rarely has guests over. Well, good for him. He should have more friends.

Let's see, what have I learned so far from this brilliant project of mine?

> *I'll never live up to a mamma-boy's mamma.
> *Gay boys usually prefer other gay boys for romantic relationships.
> *Men who want large families won't stay with a woman-child who can barely mother herself.
> *An actor will never love you as much as they love themselves.

But what have I learned about me? What can I do differently to have a successful relationship? To attract the right kind of guy for me? I haven't a clue.

I sit on the sofa and think about taking a nap.

I close my eyes, about to drift off to dreamland when I hear more sounds coming from Simon's apartment. It's not a sound I'm accustomed to hearing from Simon's apartment. It's... could it be? The sounds of... sex?

I get up and put my ear to the wall. It's not Simon going solo, that's for sure, because I can hear the other person now, and it's definitely a *woman's* voice.

What woman? Whatever. Someone he's dating? Whatever. Someone I know? Whatever. Shrieks and moans and all the typical sex sounds are now escalating as it gets more and more intense... maybe I shouldn't listen. I start singing to drown out the noise, *Frère Jacque, frère jacque, dormez-vous? Dormez-vous?*

I reach out to put my Yoo-Hoo down on the counter, but I miss the counter by several inches and the bottle drops to the floor. The glass doesn't break, because that's one tough bottle. Practically nothing can break it. But the insides pour out, the chocolate milk making a swirly, sticky mess of a swirly design all over the linoleum. I sound out the word in my head, "lina-noliee-yum." Why is that such a difficult word for me?

The sex sounds build and build, and then finally come to a… climax. I've never heard *this* Simon, first hand or second hand. I mean, I assumed that he does have sex, but we never really talk about it, and I certainly have never heard it. I open up the fridge again and reach into the cheese drawer for my secret stash of cigarettes.

I sit out on the balcony and have a puff. Then I cough horribly. Cigarettes are disgusting. It's not calming me down. Pot would be a better idea, but I haven't had possession of that in years. I could go score some from anyone within steps of my apartment, this being hippie-central and all, but I don't. I put out the cig and clean up the Yoo-Hoo mess.

Well, good. I'm glad he's happy. After all, isn't that what friends want for their friends? Happiness. Yes, happy happiness to you Simon. Way to go!

My eyes begin to get watery.

Damn allergies.

Simon:

The day after. The day after is always so… weird. Like, am I supposed to cuddle her? Make her breakfast? Let *her* make *me* breakfast? Tell her I had a good time or is that too glib? Besides, I'm not even sure that I did have a good time, because I can't remember much. Although, I'm sure I did. Don't most guys? Maybe if this sort of thing happened to me more often, I wouldn't be so clueless as to the proper morning after etiquette.

We small talk our way through coffee and then head towards the elevator. The elevator doors are about to close, so I run up and put my arm between the doors, reversing the closing. We step in.

Dandy is standing in the center of the elevator, staring straight ahead.

"Didn't you see us?" I ask Dandy.

"Oh, sorry. No." She says, not looking at me. She's never not looked at me before.

Debbie clearly stayed the night, and now Dandy is not happy. Debbie said this would happen. We all stare in silence at the numbers as the elevator takes us down. The silence is painfully long, and I'm feeling claustrophobic in the elevator, even though I've never felt claustrophobic before. So maybe this isn't claustrophobia at all. Maybe it's a different kind of phobia. I make a mental note to check Dandy's phobia book later.

I can't take the silence any longer. "You going to work today?"

Both Dandy and Debbie answer at the same time, "No."

I guess I didn't make it clear to whom I was speaking. I look at Dandy, "Maybe we can … hang out?" The elevator doors open, and Dandy shoots out of there like a bat out of hell.

"Can't. Have to go to the market. I'm out of Yoo-Hoos."

Debbie bolts in the other direction, "See ya later!"

I catch up to Dandy, and we silently brisk walk together. I want to tell her that I'm sorry. I want to tell her that I wish it was her. I want to tell her so many, many things. But instead I say, "So, how did it go with the Butt Maestro (patent pending) Guy?"

Dandy looks pissed. The last time I saw her this pissed was after the *Sopranos* finale.

"So…" she says, not slowing down, "… is she your girlfriend now or what?"

"Debbie? No, no, that was just… a thing. A thing that happened."

"I didn't even know you liked her."

"Me neither. We were just out and then…"

"Please don't say *one thing led to another.*"

We're in the super market now. Dandy grabs a shopping cart with such fierceness I'm afraid she might break it.

"Well, one thing *did* lead to another. Why are you so mad, anyway? I thought you'd be happy. You're the one who's always telling me I should get back on the horse."

"That's not a horse, that's my friend!"

"A horse is a horse is a horse."

"Don't Gertrude Stein me!"

"Unless the horse is Mr. Ed."

"Don't classic theme song me!"

She takes off down the cereal aisle.

"And don't call my friend a horse. You're such a pig."

I place a box of *Cheerios* in the cart. "Okay, no more animal references."

Dandy grabs my *Cheerios* box and hands it back to me, "Get your own cart."

"But we always share a cart."

"Not today."

We shop in silence for awhile.

"Wow, you really are mad," I tell her.

"I'm not mad. You're a big boy, you can do whatever, or whomever, you want."

"Thanks."

"You have to make your own mistakes."

"Why is it a mistake? You've had sex for fun before."

"We're not talking about me."

"Maybe we *should* talk about you."

She makes a sharp turn down the soup and beans aisle. I follow her. "In fact, Dandy Day, I think I can help you with your little experiment," I tell her with more edge in my voice than I usually possess.

"I don't need your help!" Dandy snaps back.

"I think you do. Your ex boyfriends aren't your *friends*, Dandy. They're not your 'mirrors' or these huge 'lessons' or whatever else your shrink told you they are. Obsessing over your past is not going to help you with your present."

She turns to look at me, finally. "Then what? What were all of those failed relationships for?"

"To *have*. To experience. People have relationships that don't last forever. It's just part of life. That's how we learn."

Dandy continues toward the checkout stand, and I follow. We overhear a conversation two women are having.

"And the sex was incredible," one woman says.

"Really, it wasn't strange?" Says the other one.

"At first, I thought it would be. Being friends with Jake for so long, he was more like a brother to me..."

"Gross."

"But, it wasn't gross. We are both so comfortable to-gether, and we laugh all the time."

Dandy pays for her groceries and exits the supermar-ket screaming up at the sky,

"Universe! Butt out!"

Chapter Twenty-Two

Dandy:

I'm at Grandpa Joe's place, helping him in the garden. Gramps is ninety-five years old and a survivor of many things. He's a tell-it-like-it-is kind of man that I'm fortunate enough to be related to. I think he did a pretty good job raising me. I mean, sure, I'm kind of a mess in some ways, but not in irreversible ways. At least I don't think so. The one thing he made sure of was that I always felt safe and loved. I don't know if he consciously set out to make me feel those things or if those things just naturally occurred, but either way, it's how I felt. I know that Gramps will always tell me the truth. I love him for that.

"Mind your own beeswax!" Grandpa Joe snaps at me.

"But… I just don't want him to get hurt. Debbie is a heart-breaker. Don't you think I owe it to Simon, as his best friend, to warn him?"

"No, I do *not* think that. Not even a little bit do I think that."

"Well, how about Debbie? Should I tell her how fragile Simon is?"

"Simon, he is not so fragile." He laughs, as he pulls a handful of weeds. "Pull! Pull more!" He directs me. I pull weeds.

"What do you mean, he's not so fragile?"

"I mean, inside that boy, there is a real mensch struggling to get out."

"Well, I never saw his mensch."

"Why should you see it? You never look. Pass me the soil and that plant."

I pass him the soil and a little tomato plant. Grandpa plants the tomato as I ramble. "Maybe I'm worrying too much. Being too maternal. Although Brent said I wasn't maternal enough. What do you think?"

Gramps pounds the soil in. "This tomato plant here, you know what they call it?"

"No."

"They call it *Champion*. This little plant, she does very well in this area. It makes delectable fruit, abundantly all year long," he says proudly.

"That's great." Not sure why we're talking about a tomato right now.

"It *is* great. And you know, this *Champion,* she never asks the question "why do I grow very well in this area and make delectable fruit abundantly all year long? Do you know why she doesn't ask that question?"

"Because tomatoes can't talk?"

"Hand me the watering can."

I hand him the can. Grandpa waters his new plant. "Because… it is in its nature to grow. That is what it will do. With a little sun, a little water, a little love, it grows, yes?"

I smile. "So, you think I ask too many questions, and I should just… grow?"

"That's my boobila!" He pinches my cheek and then takes off for another area of the garden that needs weeding. "Pull! Pull!" He instructs me.

"It's just… without asking questions, how do you find the answers?"

"You find, you find. Have a little faith."

That's like telling me to have patience. Tell me all you want, I still don't know how to have it. After I moment, I ask Gramps, "Did you know right away that grandma was the one for you?"

"Did I know? In my time we didn't think so much. We wanted to be with someone, we were with someone. If we didn't want to be with someone, we weren't with someone. We got married. We had children. We lived our lives. Not so difficult. We didn't have so much… *psychology* back then."

"Do you think I made Kevin gay?"

"We didn't have so much gay either."

"Gramps, there have always been gay people. They just didn't talk about it because they were afraid of being persecuted."

I can tell I hit a nerve with the word persecuted. Gramps looks down at his concentration camp tattoo and rubs it and nods his head in agreement.

"Listen, Dandy, boobila, rest your mind a little," he says, as he throws a handful of dirt at me and laughs that big belly laugh of his. "Let your heart do some thinking now, yes?"

Chapter Twenty-Three

Debbie:

I've always been a fly-by-night kinda gal. A good-time-girl with no desire to settle down. I never dreamed of wedding gowns and happily-ever-afters. I was just going to live my life however I wanted, without being trapped into a domestic prison, and without having to answer to anyone.

When I met Dandy and Simon, it was like we were destined to be friends. The three of us, stuck in our arrested development together. We didn't judge one another, because we were enough *like* one another to not really 'go there.' We all seem to be at least a decade behind in our emotional development. That is, until now. Today, everything changes for me.

I arrive at work and I spot Dandy holding a tray of food. I want her to be the first to hear the news. "Dandy! I'm getting married!"

She drops the tray of food. I really should have waited until she put the tray down.

"What the hell are you talking about? He can't be that good!" She responds in such shock, she ignores the cheeseburgers and chili fries that are now resting on top of her feet.

"He's better than good, he's *the one*!" I chirp as I skate into the kitchen.

Dandy follows me. "I can't believe this! This isn't happening."

"Believe it. It is. And I have you to thank."

"No, I will not permit it!" Dandy seems serious.

"Ha ha, very funny." I decide she must be kidding around, so I just keep talking, "I have you to thank because when I saw how jealous you were the other day in the elevator..."

"I was not..."

"It made me think that I'd much rather *admit* to feelings that I might have for someone than just allow my life to pass by me and keep all of my feelings inside. Even the jealous ones."

Dandy looks like she might cry. I guess she's super happy for me. Awww.

"You see, Dand? *Your* holding back taught me to move forward."

"Great, that's just great. I'm so glad I could be of service to so many! Well if you want my blessing you most certainly don't have..."

"Me and Angelo are moving to Hawaii!" I blurt out.

"*Angelo?*" Dandy asks confused.

"Oh, wait, you didn't think that me and…"

I laugh, but Dandy looks like she might punch me in the nose, so I stop laughing and explain.

"After Simon called me by your name for the third time, it got really weird."

"Simon did what?"

"He didn't tell you? We did some tequila shots when we got to his place and got pretty trashed. He's not much of a drinker, is he? Strange, because being a bartender, I figured he could handle his liquor. Anyhow, we were kissing, or more like *I* was kissing *him*, and he kept saying your name. The third time he did it I finally said, "*I'm not Dandy. I'm Debbie!*" And he looked at me and said, "Oh. Hey, Deb." Then I said, "Hey, Simon." Then he passed out.

"But I heard you!"

"Heard? Oh, the sex sounds? That's just something from my bag of tricks. A DVD of *Debbie Does the Valley*. Different Debbie. Same valley."

"A porno?"

"No, it's the new Pixar flick. Yes, a porno. I have a little bit of everything in my bag of tricks. Ever since *50 Shades of Grey* I've had to stock up on extras though. And leather is pricey."

Dandy seems surprised, but I can't pause to think much about it, because I want to tell her the real news.

"So… back to Angelo… it was the greatest thing. I was picking up my check the other day, and I ran into Angelo. We had a few drinks, and we talked for hours. We're so much alike, it's uncanny."

After a few moments, Dandy finally snaps out of her shock and smiles. She opens up her arms to hug me, "I'm so happy for you, Deb." We hug.

"We're getting married next month in Maui. His cousin owns a restaurant, and we're going to help him run it."

"So, I guess you got over your fear of divorce?" Dandy says.

"That fear sort of evaporated on its own. I started thinking about it, and I realized that some people really do stay together."

"I've been thinking about it, too," Dandy says. Then she goes off on a little tangent.

"Like, Paul Newman and Joanne Woodward. Barack and Michelle. Mike and Molly. Sid and Nancy. Okay, they were totally screwed up, but they still loved each other. Then there's Bonnie and Clyde - criminal but in-love. Harold and Maude. True, she, spoiler alert, kills herself in the end, but that had nothing to do with her love for Harold. Maude even tells Harold, after he professes his love for her, 'That's wonderful! Now go out there and love some more.' Now, that's real love, right?"

"Yes," I agree. "Real love is real. Happy couples… happen."

"Congratulations, Debbie," Dandy beams. Angelo comes over and joins in the love. "And a Bravo to me too, si?" The three of us are now in a group hug in the kitchen.

Angelo kisses me in that group hug while Dandy tries to wiggle her way out. Soon she gives up and plants some kisses on our cheeks. It's a lovefest at the café.

Bellissimo!

Chapter Twenty-Four

Dandy:

On my skate home from work, I have plenty to think about. If someone like Debbie can make the leap into real love, why can't I? Maybe I'm so mistrusting of people that I make sure to only choose men who are wrong for me, so I know it can't go any further. Maybe I don't think I'll be a good wife. What is a good wife, anyway? (I watched the TV show, but I still don't know.) I can be loyal. I can be loving, friendly, supportive. Is there other stuff? If so, what is it, and where do I learn about it? I never got to experience a mom and dad and their couple-dom. I know gramps and grandma loved each other, but I didn't get to witness it.

But I did have all sorts of examples on television. Reruns of *The Brady Bunch*, showed me that Carol and Mike got it right with their second marriage with all of those little pecks on the cheeks and their good natured, "Oh, yous." And how about The Ingalls on *Little House on the Prairie*? Sure, they had a lot of tough times on that prairie with way too many chores, but they still seemed to love one another oodles. Paul and Jamie on *Mad About You* were in-love in that witty, tit-for-tat sort of way. But I didn't watch the last season, so I'm not sure if they make it or not. Edith loved Archie, and he was such an ass. The Huxtables were super in-love *and* super successful! Love abounds in TV Land and in the real world, right?

Right.

Then why not for me?

What am I doing wrong?

I notice Simon loitering outside of our apartment building. Is it still called loitering if it's your own apartment? Anyway, I can't talk to him right now. I'm not sure what to say.

As I skate up to the front of our building a crazy dude on a skateboard bumps into me. "Hey, watch it!" I yell. "Screw you!" The guy yells back, flipping me the bird.

Much to my surprise, Simon, a lifelong pacifist, beings to *chase him screaming*, "Hey, asshole, what do you think you're doing?!"

"Simon! I'm fine!" I assure him.

He ignores me and runs faster than I've ever seen him run! In fact, I don't think I've *ever* seen Simon run. We would always fudge our way out of P.E. class. He once told our Jr. High School coach, Ms. Collings, that he had cramps. He saw that it worked for me, so he just copied me. Ms. Collings got such a big laugh out of that she let him skip class.

Simon drags the skateboarder by his shirt and brings him to me. I had no idea Simon was so strong.

"Don't you have something to say to the lady?" Simon says, as he thrusts the guy in my direction.

The guy, unable to move his head up from Simon's strong grip, mumbles, "I'm sorry."

"Good boy." Simon releases the guy, and he skates off quickly.

"Wow, Simon. I've never ... I don't know... just... wow." I was impressed.

"You're welcome," he says as he makes his way to the elevator and holds it open for me.

I get in.

"Do you still have that pepper spray I got you?" he asks me.

"No, you ran out of cayenne pepper last month so we used it for your stir fry, remember?"

"I'll get you another one."

I'm a big girl, and I can take care of myself, but I must admit that this momentary display of machismo does not bother me one bit. Not one bit. Still, I'm not sure why he's being so nice, but then I remember, he's always so nice. Nicer than I am. "Hey, your girlfriend is getting married." I tell him.

"Who?"

"Debbie. To Angelo. They're moving to Hawaii." I study his face for a reaction.

"Well, tell her I said mazel tov," he says calmly, as if I just told him who won the Super Bowl. He's not very sporty.

He's staring at me like he wants to say something important. The elevator doors open, and I'm out of there. He yells after me, "Hey, it's Friday night. Since we're not working, do you wanna come over and watch a movie with me later?"

"I'm super busy tonight."

"Oh, okay. Yeah, me too," he lies back to me, as the elevator doors close.

Later that night…
Simon:

Okay, so she's "super-busy" tonight. Maybe she tracked down another ex and is too embarrassed to tell me about it, since I trashed her whole project. Maybe I shouldn't have done that. It doesn't matter. What's done is done.

Besides, I see her way too much.

I need room to breathe.

I'll just watch some TV on my own. It's not like I've never done that.

I'm sure a *Friends* rerun is on. A *Friends* rerun is always on.

Dandy:

I'm sure he knows I'm lying. I mean, he'll know I'm home, because the walls are so damn thin. How "super-busy" can I be if he hears me watching a "Friends" rerun? Whatever, I don't care. I need my space.

Simon:

I should stretch. I never stretch. I read somewhere that stretching is one of the best ways to keep your body youthful. I should really get into a stretching habit. Okay, here goes. Oh, yeah, that feels good. How long has the paint been chipping off of my windowsill? I'll just pick at it a little. Nope, can't just pick at peeling paint a little, it's like pulling a thread, once you start, it's difficult to stop.

Dandy:

No clean glasses for my wine? Seriously, Dandy? Heck, I'm alone, I can drink it straight from the bottle. Who cares? Hmmm, that's good stuff. Look at that Chia pet. Only I can kill a Chia pet. Maybe it'll come back to life if I water it. Yeah, there ya go, *Cha cha cha chia.* I'll wander into the bathroom to see if there's anything interesting going on in there. Tweezers. Good, no time like the present to do some plucking. *Cha cha cha chia.*

Simon:

I'm not sure why I wandered into the bathroom. I don't have to pee. Oh, nail clippers. Yeah, my toenails are getting out of control.

Dandy:

I don't know why I'm vacuuming right now. I hate vacuuming. In fact, I totally forgot that I even owned a vacuum cleaner. It's probably Simon's. Damn, this wine is good.

Simon:

Friends episode on TV: *ROSS: But we were on a break!*
They were on a break.

Dandy:

Friends episode on TV: *ROSS: But we were on a break!*
They were on a break.

I finish off my bottle of wine. "I'm going over there," I say out loud to myself. I exit my door and make a quick left towards Simon's door, at the same moment he bounces out of his front door, making a right towards my front door.

There we are in the hallway. I can hear the *Friends* episode play out on the TV from both of our TV sets now. We just stand there, frozen for a moment.

"Do you want to come in?" he asks.

I do.

I want to.

So, I do.

Chapter Twenty-Five

Simon:

Dandy is sprawled out on her back on my kitchen counter while I make us some bow tie pasta. It's her favorite, because she thinks bow ties are cute, classy and old timey. Plus, it looks like Dandy can use some food for absorption. She's always been an adorable drunk.

"I haaaaate cooking!" she says dramatically.

"How do you know if you've never tried?"

"I can just tell. It involves concentration and the use of sharp objects. It's scary. I can't handle it. Hey, do you have any wine? Let's celebrate!" she says as she sits up, dangling her feet from the counter.

"I think you've already been celebrating," I tell her, as I pour some Strawberry Yoo-hoo into a wine glass for her.

"Hey, it's pink!"

"It's strawberry."

"Chocolate is better. Why do they even bother with this flavor?" She has a sip. "I love it!"

"Well, look at that. People can change." I smile. "So, what are we celebrating anyway?"

"Debbie's alleged future marital status."

"Alleged?"

"The car's not out of the driveway yet," Dandy laughs, strawberry Yoo-Hoo splashing everywhere. "Oops, sorry."

I clean up after her, "No worries."

Dandy mocks me. "No worries, no worries. You are always so 'no worries.' Don't you ever want to be like, *'yes, worry?'*"

Dandy finishes off her Yoo-Hoo and leaps off the counter. "Let's watch a movie!"

She runs over to the DVD cabinet and starts tossing the DVDs to the center of the room, calling each one out as she does, *When Harry Met Sally, An Affair To Remember, Sleepless in Seattle, The Wedding Singer...* Geez, these are all chick flicks!"

"You bought all of those," I remind her.

"Oh. Right. Well, I am a chick."

I pick up all the DVDs. "Besides, I thought you said that there's no such thing as chick flicks. Stories were either good stories or not good stories."

"I said that?" She says.

"You said that."

"I'm smart," she laughs, snorting a little.

"You're drunk."

"You're cute." Dandy leans in for a kiss, but I back away.

"Dandy, why don't we eat something?" I suggest as I pull on my ear.

Dandy gently pulls my hand away from my ear and calmly says, "I'm fine, Simon. I promise." She looks up at me with those emerald jade green eyes and stares right through me. In that moment, I choose to believe that she is fully present, and that she is fine. In that moment, I choose to believe it so strongly that I just… let it be.

And… we kiss.

She gets up and leads me to my bedroom, quietly. I can't believe this is finally happening after all of these years.

This is it.

The big moment.

I've pictured this moment happening so many times that I'm not entirely sure that it's actually happening or if I'm imagining it.

Dandy pulls me closer to her and kisses me again.

Oh, it's happening.

The Next Day...
Dandy:

My head is pounding. These are not my sheets, where am I? I look around and realize that I'm in Simon's apartment. More to the point, I'm in Simon's *bedroom.* I feel a breeze on my chest and look down. I'M TOPLESS. WTF?! Did we? Did I? With Simon? Oh, crap.

Simon:

I'm swinging on a swing set at the park next to my ten year old niece, Ashley. She agreed to meet with me, even though she has a very busy schedule. She skipped ballet and might be late for chess club, but, her mom, my sister, could tell by my voice on the phone that it was an emergency. Ashley has heard my story and is now processing it all.

"I mean, maybe she just kissed me because she had too much wine," I say.

"Yeah, grown-ups do stupid things when they have too much wine," she agrees.

"So, you think it was stupid for her to kiss me?"

"I think she loves you."

"Impossible."

"Why?"

"Look at me."

"What's wrong with you?"

"Well, sure, I'm cuteish on a good day, like a teddy bear or a puppy but Dandy is... she's..."

"Too hot for you?" Ashley finishes my sentence.

"Yeah and smart and funny and... well, if she wanted a teddy bear or a puppy, she'd just get a teddy bear or puppy, you know?"

Ashley sighs. "Uncle Simon, you really need to work on your self esteem. Just take her to the movies, put your arm around her, and tell her that you like her more than a friend. What's the big deal?"

"The big deal is that I could be rejected. The big deal is that I won't be rejected, and we will get together, and it won't work out. The big deal is I would lose my very best friend."

Ashley stops swinging. "How did you get to be such a big wimp, anyway?"

"Somehow that comment is not helping me."

"It's called tough love. I saw it on *Dr. Phil*."

"I'm not a wimp. I'm just scared of losing her."

"That's what wimps are. People who are scared of things."

Ashley, clearly, is wise beyond her years, but she's also getting on my nerves right now. I mean, I think it's an understandable fear, the fear of rejection. But still, I asked for this. I showed up to swing on the swings at the park and get Ashley's counsel, and she's missing ballet and everything.

"You don't know much about girls," she continues. "She wouldn't have kissed you if she didn't want to. She's probably thought about kissing you for a long time now. Just like you've thought about kissing her. I mean, it's only natural. Boys and girls, assuming that they are both heterosexual, tend to occasionally fantasize about being with each other romantically. Even if they are just friends. They did a study. I saw it on *20/20.*"

Fine. I thought about it. But still. Maybe that's how it's supposed to stay. You know, sometimes when we make our fantasies realities - they don't measure up.

I ask Ashley, "But what if it's a disaster?"

"From the ashes of disaster - grow the roses of success."

"Where did you hear that one? The Discovery Channel?

"*Chitty, Chitty, Bang, Bang.* You should Netflix it. Listen, don't make her think that she's chasing you. Girls don't like that. Man up!"

"Maybe you're right. I should get back. She's probably waking up about now."

"*You left her alone in your place?* She's going to feel weird now! She wakes up and you're not there? You really are lousy at this stuff."

She's not wrong.

"Don't feel bad, Uncle Simon. You can't help it. You're a boy."

I get off the swing and kiss my niece on the top of her head. "Thanks, Ashley."

"Don't mention it. I like helping you out, uncle Simon," she says as she begins swinging again. "It takes my mind off of my own troubles."

Dandy:

I've been here an hour now. I thought it would be strange if I left, but now I think it's strange that I stayed. Is he coming back? It's his apartment, so I'm assuming he will eventually come back. I looked everywhere for a note but found nothing. He did set the coffee maker, so that was… considerate. Unless it's on automatic, in which case, it's not anything at all. Sometimes, I feel that my mind may implode from all the bouncing around that goes on in my mind. I went to a Buddhist meditation retreat once where they taught us about the "monkey mind." The monkey mind is a mind that can't sit still, always swinging from one branch to another. There's an entire monkey village in my mind. Okay, that's it. I think we are going to just pretend nothing happened and get on with our normal lives. But what was so great about our normal lives? I need to get out of here.

Just as I open the door to leave, Simon appears. We keep doing that.

"I was just leaving," I explain.

"Oh, I thought we could talk."

"Um, I folded the blankets and put them on the sofa and thanks for the coffee unless it was on automatic and not really for me…"

"Slow down." Simon stops me. "You don't need to freak out."

"Who's freaking out? I'm not freaking out. What's done is done. We can just put this behind us... I was drunk... we are two grown adults, things happen, it doesn't have to mean…"

"Nothing happened."

"I had too much wine, so I'm sure I was a little forward and…"

Wait. What did he say? Why didn't anything happen? I just stare at him, confused.

"We kissed. That's all." Simon says matter-of-factly. "But that's it, like you said, you had too much wine. I tucked you in."

"But, my shirt…"

"You took off your shirt. You said it was too constricting."

"Oh, that's embarrassing. "I hate button downs. I should stop buying them."

Simon smiles. "How about breakfast?"

I guess I can do breakfast without being a total spaz, right?

Chapter Twenty-Six

Simon:

On the way to the café, The Ride-By Psychic rang his little bell at Dandy and screamed, "WAKE UP!" Dandy didn't seem amused. I told her that I thought that was more of an instruction than a prediction. She shrugged and looked the other way.

We're at the café now, and Dandy is enjoying her chocolate pancakes immensely. She looks up on occasion and smiles at me. She's a little jumpy but not too bad. I want to tell her so many things. All the thoughts I've been keeping in my head since we first met that day on the monkey bars in fifth grade. She used to race the other kids to see who could get to the end of the bars the fastest. She would bet a carton of chocolate milk. If she won, she'd get the other kid's chocolate milk. She always won. Hey, maybe that's when her chocolate milk addiction began.

"Is that good?" I ask her.

"Hmmmm." She answers.

We continue like this for a bit.

She eats.

I watch.

I sip my coffee.

Not sure where to begin. Is this a beginning at all?

Maybe not. If I don't do anything.

I think about telling her something, anything, when Julie, an old friend of ours, sees us and comes over with her baby.

"You guuuys! Hiiii!" Julie squeals.

"Hey, Julie," Dandy says.

"Hey, buddy." I grab the toddler's foot and he laughs. "Gimme five." The kid gives me five.

"Impressive," Dandy says.

"Yeah." Julie tells us, "Steven makes him do that each time the Chargers get a touchdown."

"How are things with you and Steven?" Dandy asks.

"Oh, much better. We started going to therapy. Our therapist told us that we need more romance in our lives. Oh! That reminds me, we went to Long Beach for one of those Gondola Getaways."

"Didn't you date a gondolier?" I ask Dandy.

"Well, he's still at it," Julie informs.

Dandy looks at me. "Anthony. He's the last one on the list."

Chapter Twenty-Seven

Dandy:

We're back at Simon's place, sitting on his sofa, bingeing *How I Met Your Mother* on Netflix. We just watched a scene where Robin pretends to hate Barney, but of course, we know how much they love each other.

"What if we're doing it just because everyone else thinks we should and not because we really want to?" I blurt.

"We're not doing anything yet," Simon tells me, calmly. How can he always be so calm?

"We're not?"

"We're just thinking. Just talking. I mean, we kissed last night. No big deal."

Why does he keep saying *no big deal?* That's not good. It *should* be a big deal.

Why wasn't it a big deal?

"So, it wasn't any good?" I ask.

"You don't remember?"

"Sorry."

"Well, it was just a little kiss. I tucked you in and you fell asleep. Like I said, no biggie."

Kissing me is a HUGE BIGGIE! At least, it should be, shouldn't it? It should be huge and memorable.

I need a do-over.

There's so much I want to tell Simon, but I can't find the words. I feel like I'm in a dream, and I'm trying to scream, but nothing is coming out of my mouth. I want to tell him how I feel about him. How I feel when I'm with him. How I've always felt about him and what a stupid scaredy-pants I've been all of these years. There's poetry and music and so many words floating around inside of my head that I would share if I could make sense of it all, but I can't seem to share any of it. So, I decided in that moment that if I can't use my mouth to form words that I'll use it for something else.

I grab Simon and climb on top of him and kiss him full on the mouth, long and hard and like I mean it because… I do.

Then I whisper in his ear, "Still no biggie?"

Simon carries me, yeah, *carries me,* into the bedroom. He places me down on the bed, "Hold on. I want this to be perfect," he says.

He turns on some music. Dims the lights. Lights a candle. Then, I stand up and face him. There we are, in a brand new position for us. We're not joking, teasing, ribbing each other. We're not goofing around, watching TV, eating pizza, or complaining about our life.

No one is drunk and no one is on a Yoo-Hoo sugar high.

We are standing there, in Simon's dimly lit bedroom with Leonard Cohen singing *Bird on a Wire*. Simon knows what I like.

Simon takes of his shirt while keeping eye contact with me.

I take off my shirt while keeping eye contact with him.

He unbuttons his pants.

I do the same.

The tension is… tense. But I think it's sexual tension and not just tension tension, but I'm not entirely sure.

I move to kiss him again and then…

SNEEZE. Right in his face! "I'm sorry!"

"It's okay, no worries," Simons says, as he grabs the shirt he just took off and dabs his face with it to wipe off my sneeze. We take a deep breath at the same time.

Simon moves in this time for the kiss and then… *CHOKES!*

"Are you okay?" I ask him, patting his back.

"A bug, I swallowed a bug…" he manages to get out between coughs. He runs to the bathroom, where I hear spitting and gagging noises. After a while he comes back out.

"Where were we?" he says, trying to be as nonchalant as possible.

"We were here," I say as I jump on the bed in an attempt at being playful, not realizing that his chandelier hangs lower than mine does.

I *WACK* my head into the chandelier, which sends me down, *flat on my face.*

"Are you…''

"I'm okay, I'm okay!"

Now Simon is sitting on the bed where I lay face down. I prop myself up and we are, once again, face to face. This is it.

We both go in for the kiss…

"SCREW YOU, YOU SON OF A BITCH! JESUS IS GOING TO GET YOU!" Screams one of our lovely Venice Boardwalk regulars for all to hear.

I can't. I just can't.

"I think we need a break," I blurt.

"Okay. Let's relax, have a drink."

"No, I mean a real break."

"Oh."

I've always been very susceptible to things I watch on television.

Simon looks devastated. I feel bad. I try to explain, "I mean, there's all this pressure because we know each other so well. Maybe we just need… a breather."

"Whatever you need," Simon agrees.

"Okay." I get up. "I'll call you."

"Okay."

I'm putting my shirt back as I head for the door. I turn around to say good-bye to Simon, "Good-bye, then."

"Good-bye, then," he says as we hug.

The hug lasts longer than normal, and I feel like I could cry.

As Simon pulls away from the hug, he kisses me. He makes the move, with confidence, and kisses me. A real kiss. A good, no, a *great* kiss. A memorable, big deal, *biggie* type of kiss, and we are both sober and present as he leads me into the bedroom, where Leonard Cohen is now singing *Lady Midnight*.

I no longer feel like leaving.

We don't sneeze, cough, bump heads or pay any attention to what's happening on the boardwalk.

Now, it's just us.

Completely and totally us.

And it's amazing.

Chapter Twenty-Eight

Two Weeks Later...

Dandy:

> I'm a coward.
> An idiot.
> A baby.

> I bailed on Simon. When did I become so afraid? I remember when I used to jump into the water without even testing it first. When I would bravely be the first to say "I love you." But now I need to know ahead of time that the pool is heated, and I'm hoarding my next "I love you" for a time that may never come.

Simon:

> The morning after our big night she was gone. She left a note saying,
> *"Gone away to think. I need time."*

"Jeez, you grown-ups sure know how to make every-thing complicated," Ashley says. We are at *Color Me Mine* painting pottery. "Have you called her?"

"No, I told you. She said she needs time. So, I'm giving her time."

"You're the *boy*. You're supposed to call."

"That's old fashioned thinking. I thought you were a modern girl."

"Some old fashioned things are nice. I watch *It's a Wonderful Life* every Christmas, and that's old fashioned."

"Dandy and I watch that every year too," I say woefully.

"I think, like, a million people watch that movie every Christmas, so it's not so special," Ashley tries to snap me out of my funk. "I bet she's wondering why you're not calling her. Was the whoopie any good?"

"*Whoopie?* Did you hear that at school?"

"No, on *The Newlywed Game*. It was on the Game Show Channel.

It could be that we all really watch way too much television.

"Uncle Simon, you didn't answer my question, was the whoopie good?"

143

"Yes. I thought it, the whoopie, was great. More than great. It seemed... wait a minute, I can't talk about sex with a ten year old. It's not right."

"Whoopie means sex? I thought it meant kissing. *Gross!"*

Oh, thank goodness, she really is ten after all. My sister, Ashley's mom, comes by.

"Are you kids ready to go soon?"

"Yeah, mom, just two more minutes," Ashley tells her.

My sis smiles and walks to the cash register to pay for our clay pots.

"My mom says you just need a good, swift kick in the butt. She says that you say you're a writer but that she's never seen you write and that you don't take enough chances in your life and that you're really wishy-washy but that you've got a good heart."

"What do you think?" I ask my niece.

"Just go get the girl." She smiles.

Chapter Twenty-Nine

Dandy:

When I woke up the night after we sealed the deal, I woke up staring at the ceiling. I felt like Billy Crystal in *When Harry Met Sally.* That's what Harry did. Harry stared at the ceiling, while Sally got up, happily, to go get some water. Harry was freaked out. Well, I was a total Harry. I've been staying with gramps for the last couple of weeks to get my head together.

I'm at the Long Beach canal now. I finally found a day when my ex, Anthony, was on duty. When I first called, they said he was out of town for the summer, but I guess he came back early, because I got an email today saying to show up at 1:00pm for my gondola ride. So, here I am. This is my last interview. After this, I'm joining a nunnery. Except, I don't think they let Jews join nunneries. So, I'll have to think of something else.

Last set of questions to ask Anthony…

Do you think that I had any *social inhibitions, feelings of inadequacy and hypersensitivity to negative evaluations? How about excessive attention seeking? How about an acute discomfort in close relationships, cognitive or perceptual distortions, and eccentricities of behavior?*

The gondola arrives. The gondolier is wearing a large hat, with his back towards me. He motions for me to climb on board. Okay, I guess this mystery bit adds to the romance. Even though it's just me. I'm probably the only person, in the history of gondola riding, who's ever done it alone.

"Hey, Anthony, it's me, Dandy," I say, as I make my way onto the boat. He starts rowing but doesn't answer me. Maybe he's mad at me. Maybe the break up wasn't mutual. "I just have a couple of questions for you, and then I won't bother you again. I'm doing a... thing. A study, sort of."

He starts to sing, in Italian. Or gibberish. I'm not really sure.

"I don't blame you for not talking to me. My project is not terribly romantic. It's not fitting of the surroundings. Besides, I think we ended abruptly. Chances are it was my fault. So... I'm sorry about that too. But, I'm trying to work through these problems of mine." He still won't answer me. "If it *wasn't* my fault. I forgive *you,*" I add.

It's really beautiful on the water. It reminds me of the time Simon and I went on a cruise together when we were in our twenties. We would sit out on the deck and watch the water together, talking about all the things we wanted to do with our lives. That was about ten years ago. Damn it, time really does zoom by, doesn't it? On the other hand, it feels like it was just yesterday. How can it be both? Life is one confusing puzzle.

"Hey, Anthony? Remember, Simon? We're still friends, can you believe it? You used to wonder about us. Yeah, me and Simon, we were going to take a break from each other because... well, I forget why exactly. But then we changed our minds, Simon and I.

Then we slept together.

Then we stopped talking.

You don't mind if I talk to you about Simon do you? I seem to ramble more when Simon's not around. I talk to myself more when he's not around too. I guess because when we were together, Simon and I, everything just flows, you know what I mean?"

It's true: everything made sense with Simon, until I decided that it didn't. I could really be myself around him. I never worried about what he thought of me. He just... accepted me. Maybe Simon was right. It is that simple. Oh, man, I wish he were here.

He loves being right.

That's when I notice the bucket at my feet with a cloth napkin on top of it. A bottle of vino for the romantic couple, I suppose.

I remove the napkin and find, chilling in the bucket...

a bottle of strawberry *Yoo-Hoo.*

The gondolier stops singing and topples the boat over. *"HEY!"*

I'm in the water now, about to yell at Anthony, but I can't, because it's *not Anthony.*

"Simon?" We are both bopping up in down in the water now. I notice his bow tie and his smile. "But, how did you, when did you…"

"Shhh…" Simon shushes me. "It's my turn to talk now."

"But, I don't…"

Simon puts his finger to his lips and repeats, "Shhh." I shush.

Simon continues, "I remembered what the Monet poster said, the one we couldn't remember at the museum that day. It said, *Everyone tries to understand my art. But it is not necessary to understand - only to love."*

"Oh, Simon… I've been…"

"…Still shutting up." I stop talking. We continue to bop in the water, and Simon continues.

"I don't understand why you eat jalapeños like they're jelly beans or why you can't pronounce linoleum and why you drop ten things a day or why you get so obsessive about knowing everything or why I feel the happiest when I'm with you and the loneliest when I'm not. I don't care about the *whys* anymore. And you're not going to screw this up - because I won't let you. I love you, Dandy Day. I always have, and I always will."

My eyes are welling up now. "Is it my turn to talk?" I ask him. He nods, and I tell him,

"I finally found the answer to my questions. The reason why I could never make a relationship work before."

"Yeah, and why is that?" He asks, holding me close in the water.

"None of my relationships ever worked out... because none of them were you."

My notebook floats by us on the water. With the ink smearing, it begins to sink. We kiss.

"What did you do with Anthony?" I ask him.

"I told him I needed use of the gondola and his hat, because I was going to profess my undying love to you."

"What did he say?"

"He said, 'It's about fucking time, dude.'"

We laugh, and then Simon kisses me.

Looking deeply into my eyes, he quietly asks me, "Am I still like a brother to you?"

"No," I tell him. "More like a cousin."

Simon dunks me into the water.

When I come back up, he brushes my hair out of my face, and we kiss some more.

THE BEGINNING

Coming Soon!

Just a Theory
a quantum love adventure
by
Annie Wood

Just when Martin thinks his life will never go anywhere remotely interesting, he meets an eccentric quantum physicist who gives him the ability to travel to his parallel lives where, in one of them, he runs a successful bed and breakfast with his beautiful wife in Italy. Problem is, he has no control over any of it.

For more information
visit: www.SpeakingVolumes.us

Coming Soon!

Girl in the Whirl
by
Annie Wood

Laureen is an overwhelmed seventeen-year-old closet poet who gets stuck raising her two younger sisters after their flaky, actor addict dad abandons them, and their bipolar mom proves unreliable. Things get even more complicated when dad suddenly comes back after three years and wants to reconnect.

**For more information
visit:** www.SpeakingVolumes.us